"Skidd writes convincingly...the story works..."

WHITEHORSE STAR

Kids "...9 to 59 will enjoy following the antics of amateur sleuths Ashley, Jonathan and Matthew, who manage to get into more trouble than a trio of bear cubs."

Editors' Choice
Our Favorite Book Titles
ALASKA *magazine*

ALASKA HIGHWAY ADVENTURE SERIES

Volume 2

THE GREAT INUKIN MYSTERY

DAVID SKIDD

MIDNIGHT INK

Published by Midnight Ink, Palm Desert, California

ISBN: 0-9636214-1-6

First Midnight Ink printing May, 1993

Printed in the U.S.A.

THE GREAT INUKIN MYSTERY

Contents

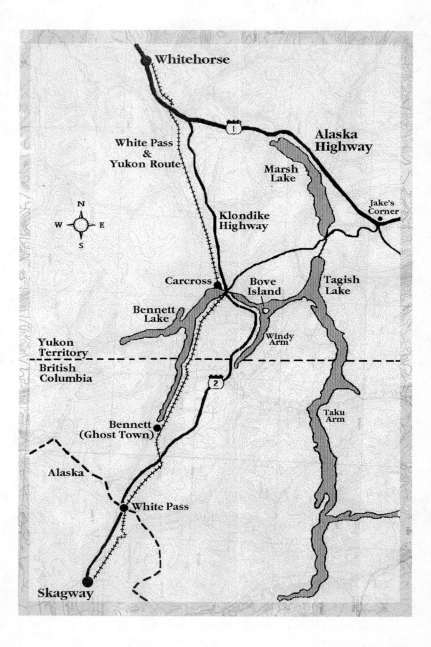

1

FLOATING BEAR

Ashley's face felt like it was being peeled back by the cold wind as the pleasure boat hit cruising speed.

She could have stood in the canopy's shelter but she didn't want anything between her and the mountains ringing Marsh Lake.

She could see her younger brother Matthew talking to Stew, the boat's owner, but she couldn't hear them over the engine's roar. This, she thought, is heaven.

Ashley's twin brother Jonathan tapped her shoulder. "Isn't this heaven?" he shouted, brushing away a tear squeezed from his eye by the bright sunlight, the boat's speed, and the wind.

It was early summer in the Yukon. The ice had

1

disappeared from the lakes but snow could still be seen between the trees and on the mountainsides. They had just left the dock and were roaring south. At this speed they would travel the twenty miles to the end of the lake in no time. Then they would enter the Tagish River and continue southward into Tagish Lake.

"How long before we reach the end of Marsh Lake?" Matthew asked.

"Depends," said Stew, a faraway look in his eyes. "Could be quick or slow. Depends."

"Depends on what?" asked Matthew. "I don't know how you could call this slow. I mean, we're really moving."

Stew glanced at his young companion and smiled. "True, but if we weren't going this fast, we'd be going slower, right? And if we went a lot slower, it would take a long time to go twenty miles in this boat, right?"

"Sure it would, but we're not going slow. You said it depends...depends on what?"

Stew's gaze returned to the water. He had retired five years ago and loved every minute of his freedom. He made his home on Marsh Lake and enjoyed introducing the three youngsters to what he called his back yard.

Matthew thought Stew hadn't heard him, so he yelled. "What does it depend on, Mr. Priest?"

"Lots of things,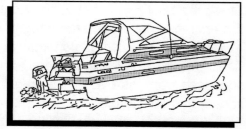

Matthew," replied Stew. "It mostly depends on whether the boat breaks down. You see, this boat is special, some say..." He stopped and looked at Matthew. "Maybe I shouldn't tell you this...maybe you're too young."

"I'm not too young," protested Matthew. People seemed to think he was either too young or too old for everything. "What about the boat?"

"Well, some say the spirit of my first wife inhabits this boat. I don't know why. We split up years before I even bought it. The boat works fine, see, until I get happy. As soon as I relax and start enjoying myself, the boat breaks down. People say it's my first wife just trying to make me mad. It works, too. Took me eleven hours to go the length of this lake once, using the small spare motor. Like I said, it depends."

Matthew eyed Stew suspiciously. "Your first wife's spirit?" he asked. "You believe in spirits?"

"Put it this way, Matthew. If you, Ashley and Jonathan want to spend the next few days camping on Bove Island, don't let me get too happy today." Stew's voice was serious, but Matthew saw the hint of a smile crease his face.

"What's happening?" asked Jonathan, entering the cabin. He rubbed his hands together to keep them warm. "Sure gets cold out there when the wind blows, doesn't it, Mr. Priest?"

"Jonathan," interrupted Matthew, "what do you think about spirits...do you think there are such things?"

"You mean like ghosts?" asked Jonathan. "I don't think

3

so. There isn't much evidence, but it's hard to say, I guess. Why?"

"Hey," shouted Ashley, "there's something in the water." She was pointing ahead of the boat, to the right. "Mr. Priest, there's something floating in the water."

Stew swung the boat in the direction Ashley was pointing and throttled the motor down quickly.

As they approached the floating object, Ashley peered at it with her binoculars. It bobbed in the small waves and looked oddly out of place in the middle of the lake. Whatever it was, it didn't belong there. Jonathan and Matthew joined Ashley at the side of the boat as they drew near. It looked like a blob of black hair. They couldn't tell what it was.

"What is it, Mr. Priest?" asked Ashley.

"Can't tell," said Stew. "We'll have to get alongside and have a closer look. Grab that pole with the hook on the end, Jonathan, and see if you can pull it to the side of the boat."

Jonathan found the pole and handed it to Ashley. She leaned over the side and reached toward the black blob. After several attempts she managed to pull it to the boat's side. Jonathan climbed to the diving platform at the back of the boat. Stew joined him and together they pulled it partially out of the water.

"What is it?" asked Matthew.

"It's what's left of a black bear," said Stew. "Not a big bear, but an adult." He handled the decaying carcass carefully.

"Excuse me," said Ashley, a pained look on her face, "that is just too gross. I hope you're not planning to bring it on board, Mr. Priest. It's repulsive."

"It's just a dead bear, Ash," said Matthew, enjoying his older sister's discomfort.

"What's it doing here?" asked Jonathan. "How did it die?"

"It was shot," replied Stew. "See the bullet hole? It's been cut, as though someone started cleaning it and stopped. It doesn't make sense. No legitimate hunter would do this. I'll have to report it to the Wildlife Department. That's all we can do, I guess." He started to shove the carcass back in the water when Jonathan noticed something.

"Hey," said Jonathan, "what's this on its ear, this metal thing?"

Stew turned the bear's ear and saw the tag. "Good eye," he said. "It's an identification tag put there by Wildlife officers. They must have tagged him when he was young. Let's see if we can make out the number."

"Why not just take the tag with us?" suggested Jonathan.

"Good idea," said Stew. He clipped the identification tag from the ear with his pocket knife and pushed the bear into the water.

Before Stew could climb from the platform, they heard a sharp *crack.* A rifle shot! The sound echoed across the lake in the clear morning air.

"Hit the deck," yelled Stew, "and keep your heads

5

down!" Stew didn't think anyone was really shooting at them, but he thought it was better to be safe than sorry. He changed his mind when a second shot rang out—followed instantaneously by a dull *clang* as the bullet slammed into the metal rail just above his head.

The engine roared to life and the boat shot forward. Stew lifted his head to see Matthew steering the boat away from the western shore.

"I can see two men on shore," yelled Ashley. "They're definitely shooting at us."

"Ashley Adams," shouted Stew, "get those binoculars out of your face and get your head down." He was amazed how calm she was, considering the circumstances.

"It's cool," announced Ashley. "He put the rifle down. I don't think he'll shoot again."

Stew was at the wheel a moment later. "Good work getting us out of there," he said to Matthew. "I didn't know you could operate the boat."

"Me neither," said Matthew, grinning. "But I had to do something. Dad would be upset if we let anything happen to you." The children laughed, but Stew wasn't sure it was funny.

"What do you think was bothering those buttheads?" asked Jonathan. "I felt like we were in Los Angeles."

"They sure didn't appreciate us looking at that bear," said Ashley.

"The bear must have something to do with it, for sure," said Stew. "There's no other explanation."

"Well, maybe we'll find out," said Matthew. "What a

kicking way to start a camping trip."

WINDY ARM

Their journey resumed, the four were soon winding their way southward out of Marsh Lake, under the Tagish River Bridge and into Tagish Lake.

"Hang on to your hats," said Stew as he guided the boat to the west. "We're heading into Windy Arm."

"Is it always windy on Windy Arm?" asked Ashley.

"Most of the time," replied Stew. "See those whitecaps on the water ahead? It's windy in there today."

"How long is this section of the lake?" asked Jonathan.

"Maybe fifteen or twenty miles," said Stew. "We're only going about halfway, to Bove Island. Tagish is a big lake... skinny, but long."

Just then Matthew flew up the steps from below. He was carrying his notebook communicator computer and he was obviously excited. "Stew...Stew. What's the number..."

Ashley interrupted. "Matthew, it's Mr. Priest, remember?"

"You kids can call me Stew if you like," said Mr. Priest. "What were you..." This time Jonathan interrupted.

"No, Mr. Priest. Dad has rules about that. To us, you're Mr. Priest."

"I'm sorry," apologized Matthew, anxious to tell them what he'd found. "Look, you guys. Look!" He held up the screen of the small computer. "Isn't it awesome?"

Ashley, Jonathan and Mr. Priest looked at the small screen. They could hardly see it in the bright sunlight. They turned their eyes to Matthew.

"Don't you see?" he asked, impatiently. "I got through. I got through!"

"Radical, dude," said Jonathan in a deadpan voice. "So tell us. Where did you get through *to*, Matt?"

"I'll show you," said Matthew. "What's the number, Ste...uh, Mr. Priest? What's the number?"

Stew loved these kids from California. The thing he liked best was that they were always surprising him. They were always doing something interesting. Sometimes, though, he couldn't figure out what they were doing—like right now. "What number?" he asked, bewildered.

"The bear's number...from his identification tag."

Stew took the tag from his pocket. "Looks like 406 to me. What do you think, Jonathan?" Jonathan looked at the tag and confirmed the number. Matthew was already tapping the communicator's keyboard.

"Matthew, what are you doing?" asked Ashley.

"There it is...I have it. Man, this is so awesome."

The others decided to wait for Matthew to explain. They were used to him going off into his own world and knew he couldn't be rushed.

"Here it is. That bear was a male black bear born four years ago near Two Horse Creek. His range covered the area between Two Horse Creek and the western shore of Bennett Lake. See, they have his weight when he was tagged, how many teeth he had, his health...everything.

This is great stuff."

"Ashley," said Stew, "could you or Jonathan explain to me what he's done and how he did it? Is he actually reading from the computer files at the Wildlife Department?"

"That's what he's doing," replied Ashley. "Someday we'll be visiting Matthew Adams in jail."

"Yeah," laughed Jonathan, "and his cell will be right down the hall from Ashley Adams' cell."

"I don't do it anymore," blushed Ashley. "It's kid stuff."

"Sure," replied Jonathan. "Now that you've taught Matthew everything you know about hacking, you get him to do the shady stuff," he said with a grin.

"Where's Two Horse Creek and Bennett Lake, Mr. Priest?" Matthew asked.

Stew guided the boat so it crossed the waves at a safe angle. The wind was getting stronger and the boat hit the water with a steady *thump, thump, thump.*

"Hold on a minute," said Stew. "How can you be reading those files on a computer in Whitehorse when we're in the middle of Windy Arm? Is that some kind of extrasensory perception computer, or what?"

They laughed. It was a fair question. How could Mr. Priest know their father's friend in Palm Springs had given them a new model to test?

"I thought you had to connect a computer to a telephone to do that kind of thing," said Stew.

"You do," said Ashley, smiling. "There's a cellular phone inside."

"Where did you get the number to dial?" asked Stew.

"I called and asked," replied Matthew. "What's neat about this computer," he continued, "is that it has a built-in modem and cellular telephone. It also has a fax machine. I can print this information on paper if I want to. I'm hooked up to the computer by cellular phone right now. So where's Two Horse Creek?"

"Well," said Stew, "if the information's accurate, something's wrong about that bear. Two Horse Creek and the west side of Bennett Lake are a good distance west of here. That means the bear was quite far from his normal range. It doesn't add up. Nothing about that bear seems right. It's a mystery."

2

TAGISH SCRAPER

By the time they had finished setting up camp, their anticipation of exploring Bove Island overshadowed the mystery of the floating bear. Setting up a good camp took effort, but they eventually had their gear unloaded, the tent set up and a pile of firewood gathered. It was late afternoon when Stew settled by the fire and watched Jonathan wrap potatoes in foil.

"Baked potatoes for supper," said Stew dreamily. "You kids sure know how to camp."

"Not!" said Jonathan. "We're having fried potatoes and omelets. With lots of butter."

"Bad for your heart," cautioned Stew. "You should know that, seeing how your Dad's a heart surgeon. Don't suppose he'd approve."

"It was Dad who taught us how to cook" noted Ashley, tossing a log on the fire. "You know, that's something I've noticed. People don't always live according to the rules of their professions. Dad's friend, who's an investment advisor, is really successful telling other people how to manage their

money. But his own money...that's a different story. Dad says he's always investing in risky ventures and losing his shirt. I think what people say and what they do often don't match."

Matthew wandered back into camp. "Looks like other campers have been here," he observed.

"People sometimes camp here," said Stew, "but not often. You probably won't see anyone. Wish I could stay with you for a few days. Weather's good and I know you're going to catch some big lake trout." He pointed to a spot not far from shore. "Take the boat and troll. Leave your line in the water and go slow. I've pulled in some big ones there. Did I ever tell you about the time I was with my buddy Red..."

He stopped in mid-sentence, watching Matthew twirl an odd-shaped stone in his hands. "What's that?" he asked, leaning toward the boy. "It looks interesting."

"Yeah," said Matthew, gazing at the object. "It sort of

looks like the point of a spear. I picked it up back in the trees. Do you think it's a real spear point?"

Stew studied the object carefully. "It looks like an old scraper. Look how the edges are chipped away making a sharp, rounded blade. It's made of flint."

"What's a scraper?" asked Ashley.

"The Natives used them long ago to scrape animal hides. It's sort of a primitive knife. They scraped the fat off the hide and sometimes the hair, too. It was part of the tanning process. This is a real find, Matthew."

Matthew ran to the tent to get his computer. A few moments later he poked his head outside and asked if anyone had seen it.

"Maybe it's still on the boat," suggested Ashley.

"Nope," said Matthew, pensively, "I carried it off the boat really carefully. I remember."

"Read my lips, kid," said Stew, "memory can fool you big time."

"I *know* I did," insisted Matthew. He ducked back into the tent. A few moments later he returned to the fire and sat down—computer in hand. "Slick trick, Ashley," he said quietly. "When a bear attacks our tent tonight and you can't find the rifle, don't ask me where it is."

Ashley and Jonathan stared at their younger brother. "Matthew," said Ashley, "honestly, I didn't touch the computer. Where was it?"

"Under your sleeping bag," said Matthew, not looking up.

Ashley looked at her twin, a question in her eyes.

"Jonathan?"

Jonathan knew Matthew was upset. He didn't want to make matters worse by questioning Matthew's belief that someone had purposely hidden the computer. He met Matthew's stare head-on.

"Matt, you know we don't play games like that. We also know if you say the computer was moved, then it was moved. The fact is no one knows how it happened. Maybe we'll figure it out, maybe not. Like that black bear in the lake today. Maybe the Wildlife Department can figure it out, maybe they can't. So don't get stressed."

"All right," said Matthew, his mood immediately returning to normal. "Let's do an encyclopedia search. What tribe of Indians lived here? And how ancient do you think the scraper might be? A hundred years?"

The others laughed.

"A hundred years? Are you kidding?" asked Ashley. "Try hundreds, maybe even thousands of years. Right, Mr. Priest?"

"OK, OK," said Matthew. "Let's say five hundred years. What tribe?" He waited a moment and looked up when no one answered. "Mr. Priest," he prodded, "what Native tribe lived around here five hundred years ago?"

"Haven't got a clue," replied Stew. "Wait a minute. Try Tlingit."

"Aren't the Tlingit a coastal tribe?" asked Ashley.

"Got it," said Matthew. "Inland Tlingit...whoops, maybe it's not Tlingit. It's...well, what do you know? The tribe that lived around here had a lake named after it. Can you guess?"

"Tagish," guessed Ashley. "The Tagish tribe!"

"Right. Ten points for Ashley," said Matthew. "You're right, too, Mr. Priest. It *is* a scraper. There's a picture right here. See?" He passed the small computer to Stew. A sudden gust of wind fanned the fire's flames.

"Wow," said Jonathan. "Mr. Priest, if that wind is a sign of things to come, maybe you'd better get going."

"I think you're right," said Stew. He looked across the lake. "Funny, the lake looks calmer than it should be with a wind like that."

"There's a lot of information here about the Natives," said Matthew as he scanned the computer screen. "What do you guys want to know?"

Another strong blast of wind threw embers from the fire and shook the walls of the tent. Stew decided to leave before the weather became a problem.

"I'm on my way," he said, rising from his seat. "You kids be careful. Remember how dangerous the wind can be if you're out in the boat. Don't forget to wear your floater coats. I'll be back at the end of the week to pick you up. Do you have everything you need? Got plenty of matches?"

"We have at least four ways of making fire," said Jonathan. "Two kinds of matches, a butane lighter..." Matthew interrupted.

"Make that five ways," he said. "There's a picture here of a drill used by the Natives to make fire. There's a lot of neat..."

15

He was cut off by a third, stronger gust of wind blowing through their campsite. Stew headed for his boat. As he climbed aboard, he wondered where the wind was coming from. The lake seemed calmer than usual.

HIDE AND SEEK

After eating, things were organized to be ready for the morning. They inflated the boat, cleaned the motors, and checked the gas tanks. They used two small motors rather than one big one because the big one was difficult to carry. 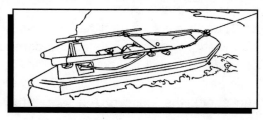 Besides, if they had problems with one motor, there was always a backup available. They loaded their tackle boxes and assembled the fishing rods. Finally, they settled by the fire.

"This isn't a very big island," noted Ashley, a map spread in front of her.

"Yeah, it's pretty small," agreed Jonathan. "Matt said it's bigger than it looks on the map, though. He walked toward the middle for half an hour and still couldn't see the other side."

"Well, if we get bored here, we can use the boat to go across to the shore," said Ashley. "It's not far."

"Has anyone seen the walkie-talkies?" asked Jonathan. "I need to put the batteries in."

"On top of the box behind you," said Ashley, not looking up from the map.

Jonathan looked at the box. He opened it and looked inside. No walkie-talkies. "Which box, Ash?"

"There's only one box, Jonathan. I put them on top of it," said Ashley. "You know, guys," she continued, "it's only nine o'clock and it won't get dark until one or two in the morning. I don't think I'm going to be able to sleep for a while. These long northern days really mess up your internal clock."

Jonathan was perplexed. Where were the walkie-talkies? He looked in the tent. Then he remembered the communicator incident. He crept up behind Matthew's seat and put his arm around his younger brother's neck.

"All right, Matthew Adams. Tell me where you hid the walkie-talkies or I'll feed you to the bears."

"Yow," squealed Matthew, "let me go. You promised you wouldn't do that any more. *Let me go!*"

"Tell me where you hid them. Then I'll let you go."

"Ashley, tell this child abuser to take his hands off me," pleaded Matthew.

Jonathan tightened his hold slightly. "The walkie-talkies, Matthew. Where did you hide them?"

"I didn't touch them...I swear," said Matthew. When he saw Ashley looking at him, he couldn't resist a small grin. "I swear!"

Jonathan released his grip. "Where are they, then?"

"I don't know," insisted Matthew.

"Did you look under my sleeping bag?" asked Ashley. She went to the tent. She was in and out in a flash, walkie-talkies in hand. "Under my sleeping bag," she said, a suspicious tone in her voice. "Matthew?"

"You're playing a new game of hide and seek, right?" said Matthew. "Either that, or maybe this island isn't a great place to camp."

"It's spooky," said Jonathan. "Let's see if anything else isn't where we thought."

"Oh, right," said Ashley. "You two probably cooked this up to try and frighten me. Well, it won't work. This is a perfectly good place to camp. Just quit hiding things under my sleeping bag."

"No, Ash, we didn't cook this up," said Jonathan. He looked serious. "Let's sit by the fire quietly for a while and see if we spot anything weird. We'll just sit here and watch."

The logs in the fire crackled and snapped in the cool summer evening. At first they couldn't really hear anything, but soon the absence of their own voices allowed their ears to channel surf to a new frequency. They all seemed to hit it simultaneously. The soundtrack of the Yukon summer burst into their island camp.

"Wow," said Matthew, "this is awesome. The quiet is so full of noise."

"Shhh," whispered Ashley. Her words were blown away by a gust of wind that shook the tent and the trees behind it. Smaller trees bent almost parallel to the ground. The wind stopped as suddenly as it began. They looked at each other in disbelief.

"Listen," said Jonathan. "There's not a sound. This place is warped. Where's the wind gone?" He looked around...nothing was moving. There wasn't even a hint of a breeze.

"Maybe it's spirits," said Matthew, quietly. He turned the flint scraper in his hand. "The Natives believed in spirits...maybe I should have left this where I found it instead of picking it up."

"It's eerie, and it isn't even dark," said Ashley, casting her eyes across the sky. "I think I hear something...high-pitched whistles. Hear it?"

"No," said Jonathan, "I don't hear anything." Matthew shook his head.

"There's an explanation," said Ashley. "There's always an explanation."

"Yeah," said Matthew. "Spirits. Way cool Tagish Indian spirits coming back to haunt intruders." He made his scariest face and jumped toward Ashley, howling *"Ooo...Oooo!"*

Ashley laughed. "Go play with your computer. Call up the spirit program."

"Uh, guys," interrupted Jonathan. "Don't look now, but something is missing. Something *major* is missing."

"At least we know where to find it," said Matthew. "Under Ashley's sleeping bag."

"It's not funny, Matthew," said Jonathan, pointing. "Look at the lake."

They looked toward the shore as a shower of sparks crackled from the campfire. It was clear what Jonathan was talking about. The boat and the motors were gone.

3

JIM

The remainder of the evening was spent in a futile search for the boat. It wasn't under Ashley's sleeping bag.

When they finally settled in for the night, sleep didn't come easily. It was bad enough the boat was gone, but it was especially confusing that it disappeared right under their noses. How could a thirteen-foot boat just disappear?

It was midmorning when Ashley's eyes finally opened. Jonathan and Matthew still slept as she crawled from the tent. The bright sunshine made her squint—but a moment later her eyes were open wide. There was an Indian boy sitting motionless beside the fire's dying embers.

"Good morning," she said, surprised the words came

out.

"Morning," came a quiet reply. He didn't even look at her.

"My name's Ashley...Ashley Adams."

"Jim," he responded.

Ashley's mind kicked into warp drive. Was this the person who took their boat last night? Had he somehow hidden the communicator and the walkie-talkies under her sleeping bag? What was he doing on Bove Island? Why was he sitting by their campfire?

She couldn't tell if Jim was happy or sad, pleasant or nasty...he sat there like a blank. He didn't send out any signals at all. This made Ashley uncomfortable. He finally turned his eyes toward her.

"I'm verbally challenged," he said.

Ashley was now completely awake. The newcomer either was going to be a problem or he had a great sense of humor. She couldn't tell which.

"Jonathan...Matthew. Time to get up," she said loudly. "We have a visitor." She noticed that Jim didn't react to her announcement. He just sat there.

"Nice to meet you, Jim," she said. "It's a beautiful morning, isn't it?" Casting her eyes into her Yukon surroundings, she immediately saw the boat. "Hey guys, the boat's back. The boat's here!" She ran toward the shore, but stopped halfway and turned back to Jim.

"Jim, did you have anything to do with our boat?" she asked.

The boy, who was a bit older than Matthew and big for

his age, glanced at the boat and then at Ashley. "Never saw a Zodiac with two motors before," he said.

Ashley wasn't in the mood for games. She moved closer. "Last night that boat disappeared," she said. "Did you have anything to do with it, Jim? If you did, I want you to know it wasn't funny."

The boy lifted his unexpressive face to look at Ashley. "Awesome," he said, his voice quiet. "I don't think you're verbally challenged. You're lucky."

"The boat...the boat, Jim. Did you take our boat?"

"Maybe I'm genetically challenged, too," he said, glancing at the boat. "Or culturally challenged. Could be lots of things."

Ashley gave up and went to check the boat. Everything was there, just as they had left it. Gas cans, fishing rods, tackle boxes, oars—it looked like the boat hadn't been touched.

Jonathan and Matthew introduced themselves to Jim. They had heard Ashley's one-way conversation and were on their guard.

As Jonathan made breakfast it became clear that Jim had something on his mind. Jonathan was determined to learn more about this stranger with whom they were apparently sharing the island.

"So, where are you from, Jim?" Jonathan asked.

"From? Now there's a good question," he replied. "Wish I knew." There was a wistfulness in his soft voice.

"He means what town or city?" said Matthew. "You don't live on this island, do you?"

"Yup, I live on this island," said Jim. "This is my island and this is where I live. I'm from this island."

Jonathan, Ashley and Matthew exchanged glances. What kind of camping trip was this turning out to be? "How long have you lived here?" persisted Jonathan. "Does your family live here, too?"

"Let's see," said Jim, looking across the lake to the mountains rising from the far shore. "Let's see...been living here for centuries. Came here two days ago. I don't have any family. My father kicked me out. Maybe I'm generationally challenged."

"Where does your Dad live?" asked Matthew. He thought the Indian boy was a bit strange, but he also thought he was interesting.

"In Carcross," said Jim. "He got mad and kicked me out. So now I live here. Alone. Except for you guys. I guess that makes me geographically challenged, eh?"

"You don't sound verbally challenged to me," said Ashley. "What's with all the challenged stuff, anyway? Sounds like you're the same as the rest of us...life challenged."

Jim looked at Ashley. "Yeah, I'm life challenged, too. Maybe I should write this down. I've never figured so much out in two days in my life. This is awesome. Do you have a pen?"

Jonathan decided Jim didn't represent a threat. "Listen, Jim," he said, "we're happy to meet you. Problem is, strange things have been happening since we started this trip. For example, last night our boat disappeared and now it's back. Stuff was moved from one place to another. Did you have anything to do with it? We just want to know what's going on."

Jim was silent. He didn't look at Jonathan. He seemed to be working through the question.

"I think I'm caught in some kind of middle," he said, thinking out loud. "And the middle is empty, know what I'm saying? I'm a Tagish Indian, but not many people know what that is, so they can't teach me about it. At school they teach me stuff, but I don't know what it's for. So I came here to live and then you guys show up. I'm caught in this big, empty middle." Jim paused and looked up at the others. "I'm middle challenged, I guess."

Matthew retrieved the communicator from the tent and began tapping the keys.

"What's that?" asked Jim.

"My battery challenged computer," said Matthew.

"Rad, dude," said Jim, for the first time showing an interest in something other than his challenges. "What's it for? What are you doing? Does it have a hard drive? How many megs? Is it a 686?"

Ashley and Jonathan glanced at each other in astonishment. At that moment they knew their visitor was an unusual character. They just didn't know if he would cause trouble, or not.

"You interested in computers?" asked Matthew. "This is a special one. Our father's friend lent it to us to test. It has a hot new memory chip called the 80886^{3N}—a neural network chip. It has a cellular phone that works with orbiting space satellites, a fax machine, built-in triple-jet printer, a modem and a sixpack ratpack. It holds about six gigabytes of storage. Not to mention a global positioning navigation unit so we can tell where we are anywhere in the world. It's loaded. Hey, I have something." Matthew tapped the keys intently, his eyes widening.

"What do you mean, you have something?" asked Ashley. "Were you scanning for extraterrestrial signals again?"

"When we went to sleep last night, I left the communicator on and set it to record any noises. This is awesome."

"Yow!" screeched Ashley, covering her ears with her hands. *"Matthew Adams, turn that thing off!"*

Everyone looked at Ashley. She had a pained look on her face and her hands still covered her ears. "Is it off yet?" she asked, nervously.

"It's off, Ash," said Matthew. "What did you hear?"

"What?" asked Ashley. "You mean you guys didn't hear that noise?" They shook their heads. They hadn't heard a thing. "It was loud and very high-pitched," she said. "It hurt my ears."

"I don't get it," said Matthew. "We didn't hear anything. How could you hear something? I'll play it again, this time with the volume turned way down." He tapped the keyboard.

"I hear it again," said Ashley. "It's short bunches of high-pitched bleeps like whales make. It's the same sound I heard when we were sitting at the campfire last night.

Can't you hear it?"

Clearly Ashley was the only one who could hear the digitally recorded sound. Matthew could see the zeroes and ones on the screen, but couldn't hear anything. He was perplexed.

"Can you check the frequencies of the sounds?" asked Jonathan. "Maybe that will tell us something."

"Yo. Look at this," said Matthew. "No wonder we can't hear it. It's outside the normal range of human hearing. Ashley, you can hear signals at twenty-four thousand vibrations per second. Normal hearing stops at about twenty thousand. Look at this vibration map." He passed the computer to the others so they could see the screen.

"What time was this recorded?" asked Ashley.

Matthew checked the time file. "At 3:35 a.m....when we were all asleep."

"Jim, were you sleeping at 3:35 this morning?" asked Jonathan.

Jim looked at his three new friends. Until now, he had thought he was the weirdest person he knew. Now he wasn't so sure. "Are you guys some kind of scientists, or something?" he asked.

"Were you sleeping at 3:35 this morning or creeping around?" insisted Jonathan.

"I was sleep challenged," said Jim, grinning.

"Does that mean asleep or awake?" asked Matthew.

"Yeah, you're right, Matthew. I was asleep, so I must've been awake challenged. This challenged stuff is a challenge, eh?"

BEAR KILLERS

For the next several hours they tried to figure out what might have made the signals. Matthew accessed databases in research institutes all over North America. Nothing they found could explain what the communicator had recorded. They thought it might have been a stray radio signal bouncing around the earth that just happened to be picked up by the communicator. But they weren't satisfied with that explanation. As for Ashley's being able to hear things she shouldn't be able to, there were no similar reports in any of the scientific studies they could find.

"Looks like we're knowledge challenged," said Jim. He'd lost his glumness and had become comfortable with these friendly California kids.

"What's this thing you have about being challenged?" asked Ashley.

"Well, it's...it's..." Jim's voice trailed off.

"It's what?" insisted Ashley.

"My school counsellor told me I was verbally challenged," said Jim, finally. "She figures that's why I don't speak up in class and stuff. I've just been thinking a lot about it, I guess."

"Sounds like your school counsellor might have a few challenges of her own," said Jonathan.

"Yeah," agreed Jim. "I think she's fish challenged, for instance. One day I took a fresh pike in for my teacher and the counsellor said it was inappropriate behavior. It..."

He was interrupted by laughter.

"You took a dead fish to your teacher?" squealed Ashley. "How gross."

"Well, there are no apple trees around here," replied Jim, smiling.

"Man," said Matthew, "I'll have to try that sometime. That's way cool."

"Jim," asked Jonathan, "do you know why someone would shoot a black bear, take it far from where they killed it and throw it in a lake?"

Jim felt good. Someone was actually asking for his opinion. He felt even better because he was sure he knew part of the answer. "I don't know why they do it," he replied, "but I know they do it. I've seen them. I call them the bear killers. They do other things, too."

"Bear killers?" asked Ashley. "You mean, like hunters?"

"No, not hunters...not normal hunters, anyway. They kill animals for some reason, but I don't know what it is. They don't eat the meat, don't keep the hide, and don't even clean the animal when they shoot it."

Jonathan told Jim what happened the day before on Marsh Lake.

"I've seen those two guys. One's short and one's tall, right?"

"Right," said Ashley.

"There's another one, too," said Jim. "A really little guy who walks funny and never talks. I've only seen him once and he didn't do any of the dirty work."

Ashley couldn't stop herself from grinning.

"What's funny, Ash?" asked Jonathan.

Ashley laughed out loud and put her hand to her mouth trying to stop. Soon they were all giggling like fools and tears were rolling down their faces. Matthew ended up rolling on the ground alternating between tears and laughter.

Jonathan finally managed to squeeze out a few words. "What...what's so funny, Ashley? What's so funny?"

Ashley was giggling as though she'd never stop. Only with great effort did she get the words out. "The third guy...the littlest one who walks funny. Jim, would you say he's...he's..." She couldn't finish the question, she was laughing so hard.

"He's *what?*" asked Jim, through his own tears.

"Would...you...say...he's...*vertically* challenged?"

Their whoops of laughter echoed across the quiet waters of Windy Arm.

Beneath the giddy laughter, Ashley, Jonathan and Matthew already knew they would soon be crossing that same water in search of Jim's bear killers.

4

UNDERGROUND HOUSE

J im explained there were two ways they could get to where he had seen the bear killers. One was to take the boat ten miles south on Windy Arm and hike eight miles cross-country to the shore of Bennett Lake. An alternate route was to take the boat west from Bove Island, through a small river connecting Windy Arm to Nares Lake, and then past Carcross into Bennett Lake.

"Since there's no way we can carry the boat cross-country, it's better to go through Nares Lake into Bennett," said Jim. So that's the route they took.

The weather cooperated and they soon neared the far end of Nares Lake with Carcross just ahead. Jim said they had to go under a railway bridge that spanned the

Natasaheenie River.

"If you guys don't mind," said Jim, "I'll sort of hunch down when we pass under the bridge so no one can see me." He pulled his baseball cap down so his face was barely visible.

"What's the big deal?" asked Matthew. "It's not like anyone's looking for you, is it? Who's going to notice you going past town in a boat?"

Jim didn't reply. How could he tell them he'd be embarrassed to be seen by his friends or his father? He'd been kicked out of his house and he wasn't about to let anyone think he couldn't handle living alone in the bush. From the corner of his eye he saw Ashley looking at him. Her quiet smile told him she understood.

The passage into Bennett Lake posed no problems for their small boat. Ashley guided it according to Jim's instructions. They all knew they couldn't have ventured this far without Jim's knowledge of the rapids and currents.

"I didn't know there was a railway in the Yukon," said Jonathan as they passed beneath the narrow bridge.

"There isn't," said Jim, "but there used to be. They built it a long time ago to carry people and supplies from Skagway, Alaska to Whitehorse during the gold rush days. It doesn't run now, though. They operate a tourist route from Skagway, but it doesn't come all the way to the Yukon anymore. It's an old steam train."

"But the tracks are still here?" asked Jonathan. Jim nodded.

32

Before realizing it, they entered the north end of Bennett Lake. It was the most famous lake in the Territory because it formed part of the original Gold Rush trail back in 1898. But gold wasn't what they were looking for today. Ashley gunned the motors and pointed the boat south.

As the boat roared along, she tried to look at all the scenery at once, an impossible task. The sky's brilliant blue collided with the tops of the mountains without warning. Where the sky and mountains met seemed like a crash site where neither would give way to the other. It was a never-ending struggle where the only winner was the observer. Ashley wondered if real beauty always had to come out of some kind of struggle between extremes. She didn't like extremes, but maybe they had a place in life after all.

The small boat skimmed across the top of the water like a turbo-charged water bug. They saw several other boats along the way, but soon they were alone. Rather than being visitors in the wilderness, they became *part* of it.

Occasionally Jim would point to a spot in the lake and spread his hands apart, indicating the size of fish he had caught there. Ashley thought his hands were farther apart as they covered the miles, but she wasn't sure.

Finally, Jim pointed emphatically to the eastern shore.

Ashley steered the boat toward it and soon they were standing on a sandy beach.

"Montana Mountain," said Jim, pointing behind the beach. "Cross five miles of nowhere, climb that mountain, go down the other side, and you're right back where we started."

"Is this where you saw those men?" asked Matthew. "The bear killers."

"Not far from here," Jim replied. "I'll show you."

Within an hour they had set up camp. The tent was up in no time, wood was gathered and a fire built. It was now late afternoon, but the sun remained high—as though it had no intention of ever setting.

"Does everyone know where they put their stuff?" asked Ashley. "If anything gets moved mysteriously, at least we'll know for sure it was moved. Then we can..." She was interrupted by Jim.

"It wasn't me, you know," he said, defensively. "I didn't even know you were on the island until this morning. I didn't touch your stuff."

"We know that," said Ashley. "You were too busy being challenged." She grinned. She hadn't laughed so hard in months as she had back on Bove Island.

Soon they were hiking away from the beach in the direction of Montana Mountain. The landscape was quilted by large open areas of scrub brush alternating with stretches of the small spruce trees that blanketed the Yukon. Five minutes from camp, Matthew made his first discovery.

"Hey, look at this," he yelled back to the others. "It's a train track."

"That's from the old White Pass and Yukon Railway," said Jim. "It runs right down the side of the lake. At the end there was a town called Bennett, but it's a ghost town now. You guys would like it."

"This track isn't normal," said Jonathan. "There's something weird about it."

"It's not wide enough," observed Ashley. "It's too little. Was the train small, or something?"

"They called it a narrow-gauge rail," said Jim. "I never really knew what that meant, but I guess it's narrower than others."

"This track is well maintained," noted Jonathan. "I wonder why they bother."

Jim pointed to a barely-visible pipe running parallel to the track nearby. The pipe was only about nine inches across. "That's a pipeline from Skagway to Whitehorse," he said. "It carries fuel oil. They use the track to do maintenance on the pipeline, so they keep the track in good condition for the crews to get to the pipe."

Matthew charged ahead. When he'd developed a good lead in an open area, he turned back and yelled, "Can you guys hear me?"

"Just barely," shouted Jonathan, wondering what his kid brother was up to.

"I'm going to try the horn to see how it works," Matthew yelled. "Are you ready?"

"Go ahead," replied Jonathan, grinning. Matthew

couldn't wait to test the air horns they had brought with them to scare off bears. The cans of compressed air were about the size of a pen, but thicker, and made a very loud noise.

"Here goes," yelled Matthew. He held up the can and pressed the top. A sharp, loud horn sound came flying across the space between them. There was no doubt it could be heard for miles.

"Could you hear it?" shouted Matthew. "It's rad! No bear will come near me."

"Oh, I'm sure," said Ashley to the others. "Now he thinks he's invulnerable because he has an air horn. When he needs to scare off a bear there won't be any air left."

"It's good to make noise as we go along, though," said Jim. "That way the bears can hear us coming and avoid us. They usually don't want trouble either."

They walked on, not fast, not slow. They weren't really trying to get anywhere—there wasn't anywhere to get. Besides, the daylight practically never ended, so why rush?

"I wish Dad could be here," said Ashley, as they worked their way around a large swampy area. "He'd really enjoy this."

"Yeah," agreed Jonathan. "I'm not so sure he'd approve of us looking for those men, though."

Jim saw the chance he'd been waiting for. "Why *did* you want to come here?" he asked. "We're not going to see those men today, unless we're lucky. I only saw them here once, and I doubt if they'll be back. Why go to all this hassle? What would we do if we saw them, anyway?"

Ashley looked at Jim as though she was surprised by his questions. "Those guys shot at us," she said. "They must have something to hide. Otherwise, why shoot at us?"

"If we find them, maybe they'll shoot at you again," replied Jim. "Why would you want that? I don't get it."

"We're here in the bush, anyway," said Jonathan. "Why not try and find out what they're up to? Besides, what's the hassle? This is fun."

"You have a weird idea of fun," concluded Jim.

"What else can we do?" Ashley asked. "If we tell the police, they probably won't do anything because we don't have any evidence. Maybe we can get some evidence."

"I told the R.C.M.P. in Carcross about these guys," said Jim. "I reported that they shot a bear and left the carcass to rot and they didn't even check it out. They probably didn't believe me."

The air was suddenly split by three sharp blasts from Matthew's air horn. The threesome looked ahead but couldn't see Matthew.

"Oh, oh," said Jonathan, breaking into a run. "We'd better find him fast!"

They headed into a stand of trees just as they heard three more blasts. The sound came from a spot not far ahead. Jonathan, Ashley, and Jim were running as fast as they could while trying to watch for the bear that might be around. Within moments they burst into a clearing. Matthew was at its center waving his arms.

37

He waved excitedly. "Over here...over here!"

"Is there a bear?" yelled Ashley, nearly out of breath. "Is it a bear, Matthew?" As they approached, she could see Matthew didn't look frightened or worried. He just looked excited.

"Bear?" he asked. "Did you see a bear?"

"Matthew Adams, why did you blow that stupid horn if there wasn't a bear?" Ashley was not pleased. "No, we didn't see a bear. We thought you did."

"Better than that," replied Matthew. "I found a house...or something."

"Oh, right, Matthew," said Ashley, looking around the clearing. "You found a house! If you found a house, why can't anyone else see it? Explain *that,* Matthew Adams."

"This better be good, Matt," said Jonathan. "We thought you were in trouble. It's not funny to mess around like that."

The twins could tell from Matthew's face that he was hiding something. He was teasing. They knew he'd found something interesting.

"Yeah, dude," said Jim. "You must have heard about the boy who was always crying "Wolverine!" and then one day when a real wolverine attacked his salmon nets no one would come."

"Wolverine?" asked Jonathan. "That's not how the story goes. It was a wolf."

"I'm a member of the wolf clan, so the wolf is good," said Jim. "So I just changed the story. It's the same idea."

"You're as bad as Matthew," said Ashley. "All right,

Matthew of the airhorn clan, where's this so-called house?" She looked around carefully. There was nothing to see except scrub brush.

"Look again," teased Matthew, grinning from ear to ear. "Whoever finds it gets ten points."

"You probably found it in your communicator," said Jonathan. "I worry about you sometimes, Matt." But he, too, looked around with more care.

Jim approached a spot where a grizzly bear had dug into the side of a low mound of earth searching for insects. "You don't mean this hole, do you Matthew?" he asked. "This is just a mess a grizzly bear made. It's not, like, where he lives or anything."

The others gathered at the hole. Dirt was scattered everywhere around a two-foot opening. Matthew couldn't hold back any longer.

"Look closer," he said. "See anything peculiar?"

The others crouched down. Ashley scraped dirt away at the edge of the hole. She noticed there was a log embedded lengthwise in the ground. A few inches closer to the hole she found another log, but it was deeper than the first one. Then she found a third and a fourth log.

"Steps," she said. "Steps going down into the hole." She hardly realized that she was already inside until she was surrounded by darkness.

"What is it?" came Jonathan's voice from behind. "What's down there, Ash?"

Ashley fumbled in her pack for her flashlight. "More steps. This thing is humongous! Come on down here, you guys. Matthew really found something. I don't know what it is—but it looks like someone lived here."

5

CHANGING SEASONS

There was no denying Matthew had found a house in the middle of the Yukon bush. It was no ordinary house, either. Holes in the dirt floor were lined with stones and looked like ancient fireplaces. Along the sides were sections separated by stones piled two feet high. It looked like groups of people, probably families, once lived in the sections.

"Outstanding," said Matthew, his eyes straining to take in the strange surroundings.

"You hit the jackpot this time, Matthew," breathed Ashley. "This is...creepy." She stood rooted in place, her flashlight pointing to the ground at her feet. She felt like she was trespassing in someone's home. It was as though

41

she could feel the heartbeats of the people who once lived here.

"Is this the kind of house your ancient ancestors lived in, Jim?" asked Jonathan. He held his arm up to the ceiling, but couldn't manage to reach it. "It's really big, isn't it?"

Jim looked at Jonathan as though he wanted to speak, but couldn't. His eyes had a slightly glazed look and Jonathan thought he looked dizzy.

"Jim," asked Jonathan, "are you feeling OK?"

"I...I'm...I'm not sure," Jim replied slowly. "This isn't right."

"You mean we shouldn't be here?" asked Jonathan, suddenly worried.

"It's not that," said Jim, regaining his composure. "It's something else. It's all wrong...this house is all wrong. But I don't know why." He moved slowly through the structure, pausing briefly here and there to touch a stone or brush his hand across a wall.

"Maybe we should leave," suggested Ashley.

"You can almost hear people talking," said Jim. "It's like someone's going to come through the door carrying caribou meat and we're all going to eat. Except it's not caribou meat. It's...it smells like salt...like the...like the ocean. It smells like the ocean. I don't think I can handle this. Could we get out of here? Something's really wrong in this place."

Ashley knew what Jim meant, and so did Jonathan. The ancient dwelling had a powerful feeling of having been lived in, but not for hundreds of years.

"Matthew," yelled Ashley. "Matthew. Let's go, we're leaving." Her voice echoed from the far end of the house, but Matthew didn't answer.

Matthew had gone on ahead. His excitement led him to follow the flashlight beam until he reached the far end of the dwelling. He, too, had a strange feeling about the place. He half expected to meet an ancient man dressed in animal skins—or even an ancient animal. But he didn't feel any fear.

Once at the end, he examined his surroundings more closely. He noticed the sections along the side walls were smaller than they were at the entrance. It looked like the house was made by people because it wasn't a natural cave. The ceiling had fallen down in places and rubble lay on the floor. He examined a small pile. Scattered before him were pieces of bone and old wood. It looked like driftwood.

Moving his light across the floor, he spotted a familiar looking piece of stone. He picked it up and wiped it clean. Reaching into his pocket, he found the ancient scraper from Bove Island. Holding them side by side, he saw they were very similar. He grinned. Dad is going to freak when he sees these artifacts, he thought, just as he heard Ashley call his name. She called again and he reluctantly stood to go.

Without warning, a furious wind blew at him and seemed to wrap him up and spin him around. Before he knew what was happening, the wind flung him from the floor straight up to the ceiling. He was spinning as if he had become the wind when he saw Ashley, Jonathan and Jim rushing toward him, their arms outstretched. They tried to grab him but they missed and he spun away. Into nowhere.

THE AHLONĒ

The wind died down and Matthew opened his eyes. He shivered. It was freezing! He soon saw why he was so cold.

He was standing outside the dwelling's entrance. Except the entrance wasn't open...it was covered with snow. He looked around, hugging himself to keep warm. Everything was covered with snow. That's when he realized the truth—*it was winter!*

The wind blasted him again. This time it was accompanied by two vague figures who grabbed his arms and pushed him toward the trees. These things aren't normal, he thought. They were a pale white color and he could see right through them. He struggled to escape their grip, but nothing happened.

What would Dad do, he asked himself, his mind racing. He looked at the figures marching him along. He couldn't say they were walking because they had no feet and left no tracks in the snow.

"Oh, right," he said. "I've been hijacked by invisible beings with no feet. Everyone's going to believe this, I'm sure."

"You should keep quiet," said one figure, menacingly. Matthew could see the figure's mouth move, but that was all.

"Radical," replied Matthew. "What else can you do to me? You flipped me from summer to winter and I'm freezing. You're dragging me through the snow and I don't know what you've done with my brother and sister, or Jim. What are you guys? Some kind of spirits?"

"We are the wind," said one of the figures. "We are the North Wind and you are our captive. You should ask no more questions"

"I'm freezing," complained Matthew. "Where are you taking me?"

The figures said nothing more. Soon they were among the trees. In time they came upon a small clearing where Matthew saw more of the ghostly figures moving about. There was a fire at the center of the clearing around which sat several more figures. Matthew was escorted to the fire. One of the figures spoke and once again Matthew could only see its mouth move.

"What have we here?"

"His name is Matthew," replied one of his captors. "He was trespassing again."

"Trespassing, were you, Matthew? Don't you know the rules?"

"You mean you hijacked me because I was in that old house?" asked Matthew.

"We are only trying to save you," replied the figure. The

voice seemed to float out of nowhere. Matthew couldn't tell if it was a man or a woman speaking. "You should have stayed with your brother and sister."

"Where are they?" asked Matthew. "Who are you? What's going on? How did it get to be winter? What are you..." His question was cut off.

"We are the Ahlonē people," said the figure. "We are the wind. You will stop asking questions or we will remove the fire that warms you." The figure paused, moving its head about as if looking for something. "Why are you blinking your eyes?" it asked. "Are you going to cry like a wailing child?"

"I'm trying to wake up," replied Matthew. "I know you're not real. I'm just having some kind of nightmare and you're in it."

The figure waved its arm and an icy blast of wind nearly blew Matthew from his feet. The fire went out and Matthew shivered from the cold.

"You doubt our power?" bellowed the figure. "Should we let you freeze? You are the prisoner of the Ahlonē people and you will respect our power."

"OK, OK," said Matthew through chattering teeth. "I respect your power. Please start the fire before I freeze. *Please.*"

"Much better."

Matthew warmed up immediately. He noticed there was no wood in the fire—just flames. Somehow he wasn't surprised. The feeling began to creep over him that he was in real trouble. These figures weren't fooling around and he couldn't wake up. If this wasn't a dream, what was he going to do? "Would it be all right if I ask a question?" he asked.

A murmur rolled through the clearing as though all the figures were talking at once.

"Very good, Matthew. Maybe you can learn not to trespass. You have earned a reward." With a wave of his arm the figure warmed the temperature considerably. It was still winter, but it was much warmer.

"Awesome," said Matthew, relieved he was no longer chilled to the bone. "Man, you're one bad dude. Can you teach me how to do that? Can you just wave your arm and change the whole season? Like from winter to summer? Or are you always in winter because you're the North Wind? By the way, Mr. North Wind of the Ahlonē people, how *do* you do that?"

The figure waved its arm and Matthew felt the gusts of wind rush in on him again. The numbing cold returned, only it was worse now.

"He is hopeless," said one figure.

"He is doomed," said another.

"He is a pain," said a third.

Matthew's heart pounded. He had made them angry, but he didn't know how. For the first time he was frightened. What was he going to do if he couldn't figure out their rules? It suddenly occurred to him that this might be his last nightmare. He felt tired and alone.

The leader spoke. "Matthew Adams, you are charged with trespassing in the Land of the Ahlonē. Though you are young, you commit many crimes. We wish you no harm, but you bring harm to yourself and to those around you. You are condemned to..." The figure stopped speaking. "You are condemned to..."

Matthew couldn't understand what was happening. The figures were agitated, whirling around the clearing without apparent purpose. The leader, until now the calmest of all, suddenly moved away and shot into the trees, as though heading for cover. The others followed, leaving Matthew alone by the fire.

He looked around. The trees were blanketed with snow, but he could hear a bird chirping. A rustling sound above caught his attention. A pair of large black ravens settled into the uppermost branches of the tallest tree. They seemed to be watching him.

Matthew didn't know whether to feel relieved or frightened. At least when the figures were there he had company of a sort...even if they were about to sentence him. He couldn't leave the fire. He felt in his pocket for matches. His hand closed around the cold flint scraper. The ravens screeched.

He looked at the scraper, rubbing it with his thumb. The wind suddenly gusted and swirled snow around the clearing. He rubbed it again, harder this time. The wind blew furiously and Matthew lost his footing. He was caught up by the wind, twirling like a leaf. He saw the fire go out just as the clearing disappeared. Squeezing his eyes shut, he hoped for the best.

"Matthew...Matthew. *Matthew*, where are you?" It was

Ashley's distant voice cutting through his confusion. "Matthew Adams, you'd better be around here somewhere. Please be here."

Matthew landed on the ground outside the entrance to the underground house. It was summer again and he heard Ashley calling his name. He carefully poked his head into the dark opening. Light from three flashlights rushed toward him.

"Hey, guys. I'm here," he yelled. "I'm here. At the entrance."

Jonathan, Jim and Ashley came into the daylight. They looked as worried as Matthew had felt moments ago. "Are you all right?" asked Jonathan.

"Geez, Matt," said Jim, "what's going on? How did you get here? You were inside and there was this big wind...and then...well, nothing. You disappeared. What happened?"

Matthew clutched the Tagish scraper tightly, afraid to rub it by accident. He slipped it into his pocket. "I'm fine...I think," he said.

"What happened, Matthew?" asked Ashley. "We were really scared. It was like a tornado in there. How did you get out here? Are you sure you're all right?"

Matthew didn't know what to say, or where to start. "You're not going to believe it...I mean, we're talking mega-weird. Can we go back to camp?"

They headed back to their campsite at the edge of the lake. High in the cloudless sky a bald eagle was gliding on the air currents. From its lofty position, it could see two

49

men, one tall and the other short, climb from a float plane. There were visitors at the camp on the shore of Bennett Lake.

6

ALASKA IN THE YUKON

As they returned to camp Matthew tried to explain what had happened. The others listened intently when he described the figures. They knew something strange had occurred, but Matthew's story was so far from their experience they didn't know what to think.

Jim couldn't make sense of it even though he was a Tagish Indian. He had never heard of the Ahlonē people. He knew some legends about spirits, but nothing Matthew described seemed to fit. Besides, while Jim was excited by Matthew's story, he was bothered by the feelings he'd had in the ancient lodge. The smell, or taste, of salt wouldn't leave him—like a song that won't leave your mind. The feeling that something was wrong about the lodge kept intruding into his thoughts.

Approaching the railway tracks near their camp, Ashley suddenly halted. "Shh," she whispered. "I hear something."

They froze. The others heard nothing. Ashley motioned for them to crouch down. "I hear men talking," she whispered. "Let's creep up on them and see who they are." She started toward the campsite. The boys followed. They carefully crossed the tracks, just out of view of the camp. By now everyone could hear the voices.

"Sounds like they're trashing our camp," said Jonathan.

They crept close enough to see the two men from behind a dense clump of willows. The camp was indeed being trashed. Camping gear was spread across the sandy shore. Their tent was still standing, but several support rods had been pulled out and it was sagging awkwardly.

"My guitar," moaned Jonathan, as though feeling physical pain. "Look at it." The guitar had been roughly tossed onto the sand.

"The communicator," whispered Matthew. "I left it in the tent. If they take it, I'm history."

"The slugs," said Ashley. "Look at them. All they know how to do is wreck things. I wish we could stop them."

"I wouldn't try it," said Jim. "Look at the rifle the big guy's packing. It's a .416...what I wouldn't give..."

"What's a .416?" asked Matthew, as the men continued their dirty work.

"A *big* gun," replied Jim. "An elephant gun. It would blow you apart. Even your Dad couldn't do surgery on you. There'd be nothing left to surge."

52

The two men, satisfied they had done enough damage, surveyed their effort. "That oughtta' be enough," said the small, slim man, reaching into his jacket. He twisted the cap from a bottle.

"No more booze," said his hulking partner. "Put the damn bottle away."

"Right," said the small man, lifting the bottle to his lips.

"You're an idiot, Roberts," said the big man in a matter-of-fact way.

"Yeah, Bongo, I'm an idiot and you're a genius. That's why I fly the plane and you make like a passenger. That's why I negotiate our deals. I provide the hustle, you provide the bustle."

"Shut your face," snapped Bongo. "I'm sayin' Wing's gonna get on your case big time if you don't take it easy on the booze. Wing don't like you half drunk all the time."

"Bongo, have I ever let us down, huh? Have I ever messed up a job? No. So shut up. Besides, Wing's just a temporary employer. It ain't like we're married, so don't get harried."

"Suit yourself. But if you keep drinkin' like that, Wing's gonna make your life temporary. That's a lock."

"Let's get back. Whoever set up this camp will think a griz came to call. They'll leave in a hurry when they see this mess, that's my guess."

The two wasted no time pushing the float plane off the shore onto Bennett Lake's calm water. They acted as though they were on a schedule.

The plane's motor hummed as the small man guided it

in a wide circle preparing for takeoff. Then, as though alive, the engine roared and the plane plowed, then gracefully skated, across the water and into the air. It soon became a soundless dot in the sky.

"What a mess," groaned Jonathan, cleaning the sand from his guitar. "This isn't exactly turning out to be a quiet camping trip."

"At least you found the bear killers," said Jim. "Or should I say they found you? Those are the guys I told you about."

"They're the same ones who shot at us yesterday on Marsh Lake," said Ashley. "They're obviously bad news."

"The communicator still works!" exclaimed Matthew. "We can call the police and report them."

"Not so fast, Matthew," said Jonathan. "Nothing's changed. Think about it. They didn't steal anything and nothing's actually broken. What can the police do, except file a report? They'll just think we're a nuisance."

"So what do we do?" asked Matthew. "We can't just let them get away with it, can we?"

"I don't know," said Jonathan, looking to his twin sister for ideas. "What do you think, Ash?"

"I think once we clean up this mess, we're going to eat. Then we'll figure out what to do."

It was early evening when they finished eating. Jim put a log on the fire as everyone settled down to consider the situation.

"If we don't call the Mounted Police," said Matthew, "maybe we could call Mr. Priest. That way someone will know what's going on. We could tell him what happened."

"Good idea, Matt," said Jonathan. "Besides, we should let him know we left Bove Island. Otherwise he'll think we're still there."

Matthew loved using the communicator's built-in cellular phone. He pulled up the unit's communication program and simply said "Mr. Priest." The machine accessed the number and took care of the dialing. After several rings, however, it was evident Mr. Priest wasn't home.

"I guess he doesn't have an answering machine," said Matthew. "Oh well, I'll try later. Anyone want to go fishing? Can we catch big fish around here, Jim?"

"Sure," said Jim, "any size you want. Arctic grayling, lake trout, or pike." Jim paused, as though framing a thought. "Matthew, could you look in an encyclopedia to find out what kind of dwelling you found? I mean, it won't leave my mind. It's like I recognize it, but I don't recognize it, know what I mean?"

"No problem," said Matthew, immediately tapping the small keyboard. "Let's see...I'll try the keywords *Ancient Native dwellings, sub-Arctic North America.* That should start us in the right direction."

"Is there anything that machine can't do?" asked Jim, marveling at the ease with which Matthew roamed the world's infoscapes. "It's like Matthew has this virtual office here in the bush."

"Virtual office, virtual library, virtual arcade, virtual reality," said Jonathan. "Where does that leave us? Like, does Matthew eventually get virtually married? Do we all end up getting virtual jobs?"

"Dad says knowing how to get information and how to use it is the secret to success," said Ashley.

"But what about wisdom?" asked Jim. "What about other things, like me and my Dad? A real father isn't the same as a virtual father. Information can't be everything. At least, well...that's how it seems to me, anyway."

"I agree," said Ashley. "For instance, Dad spends a lot of time with us, you know, traveling and stuff. And he teaches us a lot. But some of our friends, well, it's gross. They hardly see their fathers. All they do is work, come home, go to work. Then they try to cram a whole life's worth of activities into a one-week vacation. It doesn't make sense."

"What about your mother?" asked Jim. "Don't you have a Mom, either?"

"Not for a long time," said Jonathan. "Sometimes I wish Dad would get married. I'd like to have a Mom. But Dad's afraid, I think, you know, to make a big commitment. I don't know."

"Whoa," said Matthew. "Speaking of mothers, this is the mother of all houses. You won't believe it, but that lodge doesn't belong here. It's a type built by Natives on the Alaskan coast. Look at this." He showed them the pictures on the screen. "Tagish Indians didn't build that kind of lodge."

"A huge hole was dug in the ground and whalebone and driftwood were used to make a roof," read Ashley. "The drawings of the inside are exactly like we saw. Give me a break. There are no whales around here. What's going on?"

"I saw driftwood on the floor," said Matthew. "At least it looked like driftwood."

"Matt," said Jonathan slowly, "it looks like you've made a major discovery. If this is right, there are only two possibilities. Either ancient people around here lived in a way no one knows about, or..."

"Or the lodge used to be on the Alaskan coast," cried Jim, leaping from his seat. "That's why it seemed so strange. That's why I smelled salt!"

"We have to go back," said Matthew. "Definitely, we have to. We can make drawings and everything and then...and then..."

"Oh, oh," said Ashley, smiling. "Here we go. Matthew's found a project. Watch out, Jim, or you may end up working night and day on one of Matthew's projects."

"I'd like to go back, too," said Jim. "We have hours of daylight left. It would be fun."

"Why not?" asked Matthew. "If we do it right, we could announce the discovery. We could write a newspaper story, or an article for a magazine."

"Go for it," said Ashley, catching her brother's infectious enthusiasm. "Headline: *INTREPID EXPLORER MATTHEW ADAMS MAKES MAJOR ARCHEOLOGICAL DISCOVERY!*"

"Maybe I'll stay here and watch the camp," said Jim, suddenly seeming to lose interest.

"No way," insisted Matthew. "Come on, let's go back. We'll measure everything, do some drawings of the inside, write a description. Man, if that roof is made from whalebone we might even get on the news. I *love* the North."

"You two go back and look around, but be careful," said Jonathan. "I'll stay here with Ashley to make sure no more visitors wreck our camp." He knew Ashley would be comfortable if Matthew went with Jim. He also knew Matthew should be allowed to examine the lodge his own way. Their father had taught them not to rain on someone else's parade. Matt had found the ancient house, so it was his parade.

Jim and Matthew were soon back in the ancient lodge. They stood side-by-side, their flashlights moving slowly across the cold, dark, space that seemed to hide secrets from long ago.

"I wonder what it is about this place?" mused Matthew. "There's nothing here, but I get this strange feeling it's full of life...or something."

"Yeah, I know what you mean," said Jim. "It's like when you go into an old, broken-down cabin. You feel like you know the person who lived in it. Sometimes old things seem to have a person's spirit still in them." Jim paused, trying to imagine what it would have been like to live here. "So, what should we do? I can't draw, or anything, so I'll just help you."

"I can't draw, either," said Matthew. "But the kind of diagrams they use are just sketches—lines and distances and circles for rocks. It says we're not supposed to disturb things. We can measure the length and width of the lodge,

58

count the steps in the entrance, show where the firepits and rock dividers are...things like that. We'll just describe it the same way the encyclopedia people do. That should be good enough."

"How do you know this stuff?" asked Jim. "Have you done it with your father?"

"Nope," replied Matthew. "I make it up. Dad says if you use your imagination, you get to make the world. If you let other people do it, then they make your world for you. So I guess a lot. I'm wrong most of the time, but Dad says it's a good way to learn."

Working together, the two measured everything they could think of and sketched the inside and outside of the lodge. They found pieces of bone and wood on the floor and put a few small pieces in bags so experts could study them. Jim knew the names of the plants growing outside and they wrote them all down.

The most exciting discovery came when they scraped some dirt from the ceiling and measured what looked like a bone almost ten feet long.

"Wow," said Jim. "Either this is whalebone or it's from the biggest moose in the history of the planet. It's awesome."

"Maybe Bennett Lake used to be connected to the Pacific Ocean," said Matthew. "Who knows?"

"Or maybe this whole place was on the Pacific coast zillions of years ago," said Jim. "That blows my mind. I mean, it's like it can't be true, but it is true."

"I think we have enough info," said Matthew. "All we

need to do now is use the GPS to record exactly where we are. Then we'll head back."

"What's a GPS?" asked Jim.

"It's a machine that communicates with satellites and tells us our coordinates on earth. They use them for navigation in airplanes and boats, mostly. Some people use them in their cars. If the car is stolen, the police pick up the signal and follow the car wherever it goes. There's one in the communicator. It's really cool."

It was nearly midnight when the boys started for camp. The sky was dusky, but there was still plenty of light. Jim suggested they head straight for the railway tracks and follow them back to camp. "It's longer, but I like walking along the tracks," he said.

They hiked in silence. Two boys who had only met that morning now trudged together through the Yukon wilderness. An observer might think they were totally carefree, enjoying the moment without a worry in the world. But the observer would be wrong. Jim and Matthew were thinking a lot faster than they were walking.

When they reached the tracks of the old White Pass railroad, they almost walked into the side of a truck. Sitting silently on the tracks was a black pickup with a windowless black shell covering its cargo bed. The boys looked at each other in amazement. They were constantly on guard for bears and always looking for moose, caribou, foxes, wolves, and other wildlife. But a truck? Where the nearest road was miles away? No chance.

7

CARGO

The truck looked like an ad in a magazine. It sat silently on the tracks, tires off the ground, bathed in the shadowy light. Wispy orange-streaked clouds on the horizon provided a fitting backdrop for the unusual scene.

Overcoming their shock, Jim and Matthew retreated to the cover of the trees. They hardly dared breathe. As moments ticked to minutes, however, they realized there was no one around. Whoever owned the truck was nowhere to be seen.

"I've seen that truck before," said Jim. "But not on railway tracks."

"What's the deal?" asked Matthew. "How can a truck go

on train tracks? The tires aren't even touching the ground. What's it doing here, in the middle of nowhere? I don't get it."

"It's called a high railer, a special four-wheel-drive truck," said Jim. "I've seen them before, but this one is different somehow. It doesn't sit as high off the tracks. Let's check it out," he suggested, looking around to make sure they were still alone. He cautiously moved toward the truck.

Matthew wondered how a truck could travel on tracks. Peering underneath, he had his answer. "There are steel wheels under here!" he exclaimed. "Wheels just like on a train. It looks like they push down and lift the regular wheels off the ground. What a cool setup."

Jim stood on tiptoes, peering into the cab. "Yeah, I see the controls," he said. "Hydraulic system, I think."  He paused, making a face. "Do you smell anything, Matt?"

Matthew had noticed the smell, too. "Do I ever," he said. "What a stink." He joined Jim at the rear of the vehicle. Just as he turned the handle to open the truck's cap, they heard the crunch of gravel. Someone was walking toward the front of the truck. Then they heard voices—and froze.

"It's those two men," Jim whispered. "Roberts and

Bongo."

"We're stuck," whispered Matthew. "We can't get away from the truck without them seeing us."

The men drew closer. "So what if they're just kids?" asked the big man. "That don't change a thing. Wing's not gonna like the fact that they hung around even after we messed up their camp. We gotta drive past that camp and they'll hear the truck for sure. I think they might be the kids we saw on that boat. They make me nervous."

"Yeah, they might hear us go by, but what's it to them?" countered Roberts. "They won't care. They're just out camping, having a good time. It's no big deal."

"I'm tellin' you," insisted Bongo, "that girl saw us at Marsh Lake when we shot at the boat. She was usin' binoculars...she saw us, I know it."

"You worry too much," said Roberts. "Let me do the worrying and we'll be all right. If you start thinking, we'll start sinking." Roberts grinned. He enjoyed putting Bongo down. He slipped the key in the door. "Let's dump these things and get up to White Pass."

Matthew and Jim stared at each other, not daring to make a sound. As the truck's motor roared to life and Roberts released the handbrake, a feeling of doom came over Matthew. He felt like a deer caught in headlights. For an instant he didn't know what to do.

With the certainty a person discovers when he runs out of options, Matthew turned the handle on the cap and pulled the door open. The truck started to move. Without thinking, he scrambled onto the truck's bumper and squeezed himself under the flapping cap door. He tumbled to the floor. Jim was right behind him. As the truck picked up speed, the boys realized they weren't the truck's only cargo. The stench was almost overwhelming. Matthew reached his hand out to feel what he had landed on. He felt hair—like an animal's.

He swung around to face where he thought Jim was. Their heads smacked together with a harsh *clunk*. Their eyes automatically squeezed shut and they clenched their teeth, fighting the urge to yell out in pain. They managed not to give themselves away.

Their pain was soon pushed out of the way by the realization that they were in the back of a pickup truck flying down the old White Pass tracks. Their heads throbbed, but that was the least of their worries. Matthew noticed that the truck's engine and the noise from the track probably meant the men in front couldn't hear them. "Man, this place reeks," he whispered.

"There are two black bears in here," said Jim. "These guys have killed two more bears."

"Do you think they can hear us?" asked Matthew. He was facing the back of the truck.

"No," replied Jim, softly. "I can see them through the windows, but they're just talking. The sliding window in the cab is open a bit, but the one in the cap is closed."

"What are we going to do?" Matthew wondered aloud. Then he remembered Ashley and Jonathan. "Oh, no," he blurted. "Jonathan and Ashley are going to be really ticked. They'll be wondering what happened. We have to get out of this truck."

"Sorry, Matthew," said Jim, calmly. "We're stuck until they stop. We've already gone way past the camp. We're almost in B.C. now, I'd say."

"B.C.? What the heck is B.C.?"

"You don't know what B.C. is? B.C. is British Columbia. The province south of the Yukon Territory."

"You mean we're not even in the Yukon anymore? This is exactly what I promised not to do. Jim, I'm in trouble...I'm in trouble *again!*"

"I wouldn't worry about what Jonathan and Ashley are going to do," advised Jim. "We have to worry about these guys first."

The truck suddenly slowed...it was stopping. "What now?" asked Matthew. He knew they were about to be caught. It was hopeless.

"Let's go," said Jim, grabbing Matthew's arm. "We have to get out. Try not to make any noise." He opened the cap's door and silently climbed over the tailgate. He stood crouched on the bumper and helped Matthew through.

Matthew had hardly touched the bumper when Jim yanked him off and they hit the railway ties and rolled. "Keep down," said Jim. "They might not see us."

Luck was on their side. The truck slowed gradually and rounded a slight bend in the tracks. They scrambled into the trees. Jim wasn't sure what to do. They were miles from the camp on Bennett Lake, well within British Columbia. He knew they were only a few miles from the Alaskan border.

"Matt, I hate to tell you this, but we're too far away from anywhere to walk," he said. "We have to get back in the truck when it takes off. There's no other choice."

Matthew took the communicator from his pack. "I'll check our position with the GPS." In a moment the exact coordinates of their position appeared on the screen. Matthew hit a key and their position was shown on a map. It confirmed what Jim thought. They were in British Columbia.

"Couldn't we hike to the Klondike Highway?" asked Matthew. "It doesn't look that far."

"We could," confirmed Jim, "but it's not a fun hike and it's not too smart to travel out here without supplies." Jim was surprised at his own words. He realized he felt responsible for Matthew's safety because Matthew was younger than he was.

Matthew wasn't convinced. He didn't want to push their luck by trying to get back in the truck. On the other hand, he knew if they could pull it off, they would find out more about whatever it was Bongo and Roberts were up to. What would Ashley and Jonathan do? Until now, he never realized how much he depended on their judgment in tough situations.

"Let's check out what they're doing," he decided.

They crept through the trees beside the tracks. Though the sun had set, there was still enough light to work their way among the shadows. Soon they heard Bongo and Roberts.

"Damn!" grunted the small man. "Give me a hand here.

This bear must weigh five hundred pounds. C'mon, Bongo, grab the other end." They were dragging the dead bear from the back of the truck. Once they got it out, they dragged it away from the tracks. Leaving the tailgate open, they moved the truck further up the track and repeated the procedure with the second bear.

Roberts obviously didn't enjoy the strenuous work. "Let's get out of here," he said, taking a drink from his ever-present bottle. "Make sure you close the door on the cap this time, too."

"I closed the door, I know I did," replied Bongo. He hated the way his partner always treated him like an idiot. He couldn't figure out how the door had been left open. Maybe he *had* forgotten to close it.

"Let's go," said Roberts. "We're running out of time. We have to get to White Pass."

Just as the truck began to move, Matthew and Jim broke from the trees, running in a crouched position. Jim grasped the bumper, quickly opened the cap door, and hoisted himself over the tailgate into the truck. Running the risk he would be seen through the sliding window, he held the door slightly ajar for Matthew.

But Matthew didn't follow him in. With the truck gaining speed, Jim peeked out and saw Matthew getting up from the ground. Matthew's legs churned as he desperately tried to catch the black truck.

"Come on, little guy, run," Jim whispered to himself. "You can make it—*come on!*" As if it would help, he reached his arm out to his new friend and waved him on.

"Run, Matthew, *run!"*

Matthew's lungs hurt. He couldn't seem to get enough air. His legs were moving, but he couldn't feel them. His whole body was on automatic, on the very edge of control. The only thing he wanted at that moment was to reach Jim's hand, to catch the black truck. His eyes were locked on the target.

When he had nothing left, Matthew felt a hand grab his arm. He seemed to float through the air and over the tailgate. He couldn't believe Jim was so strong.

"Atta' boy," whispered Jim, excitedly. He was out of breath, too, as though he had been running with Matthew. "You made it. You *made* it!"

Matthew didn't celebrate. He just gasped for air and worried he'd been seen. Apparently he hadn't. The truck continued to roll, gaining speed.

"Wow," said Matthew, still panting. "I didn't think I was going to make it. Thanks for pulling me up."

Jim felt good. He'd never had so much fun in his life. He'd never done anything before where someone thanked him for doing what he enjoyed. It was a new kind of feeling. He was glad he'd met the Adams kids on Bove Island.

"You were velocity challenged," he said with a grin.

"You got that right," laughed Matthew. "And before that, I was...ah..."

"Horizontally challenged?"

"Yeah, horizontally challenged. My knee's scraped...I think it's bleeding. I tripped on the stupid track."

Jim glanced into the cab. Roberts and Bongo were talking...or arguing. He had an idea. "Why don't we slide the window open so we can hear what they're saying?" he asked.

In the blink of an eye Matthew crawled along the cargo bed, reached his hand up and slid the glass panel open a crack. Jim inched forward to join him.

"Sure it's a pain," they heard Bongo say, "but Wing's right. It's safer to dump the carcasses in B.C. because they won't be noticed. The B.C. government hardly monitors the area. If too many dead animals start showing up in the Yukon, people are gonna notice."

"Yeah," said Roberts, "people like those brats on the boat."

"That was one of your dumber ideas, dumping that bear in Marsh Lake. Wing wasn't real impressed." Bongo seemed to enjoy the idea that the self-anointed genius had blundered.

"Wing, Wing, Wing," snapped Roberts. "What's all this Wing stuff? You want to work with that miniature foreigner, or with me? Huh?"

"Don't get all worked up. Wing pays the bills and you know it. This is Wing's operation and we just do the dirty work."

"Maybe not for long. Maybe we should go independent. Wing's making too much money on this deal. They get megabucks for the bear paws and every ounce of powder from the gallbladders. Not to mention the birds." He gestured to the cooler in the extra-cab. "Do you realize we're carrying more than half a million bucks worth of stuff in there? Over half a million for three drugged falcons and a bag of bear gallbladders."

Matthew and Jim stared at each other. The bears were being poached for their paws and gallbladders? How could they be worth so much money?

"Don't kid yourself," said Bongo. "Without Wing's network, we wouldn't know what to do with the stuff. We don't know any Arab princes who'll pay a hundred and fifty grand for a peregrine falcon. We know how to catch 'em, drug 'em and smuggle 'em into Alaska. That's all we know how to do."

Roberts eyed his partner, wondering if Bongo was losing confidence in him. Bongo always used to think Roberts could do anything he wanted. Now he seemed to think Wing was smarter. That made Roberts nervous.

"We could set up a network if we wanted to," he said. "All we have to do is go to Taiwan, find the people who deal in the contraband, and go from there. We could cut Wing out."

"Listen to me, bro'," said Bongo, "we can't afford to get greedy. These Asian brothers don't freelance. They're tight with each other. The people in Taiwan are *Wing's* people—they won't deal with us, you know that. Their gangs go back generations, centuries. Cut Wing out and you cut your own throat. We're doin' good enough."

"Bongo, you're going soft. There's no such thing as good enough. Enough isn't an idea I understand."

"Enough," replied the big man, "is how much booze

you've poured down your throat since we came North. All that hootch is makin' you lose your neurons, man. Don't mess with Wing."

The truck steadily climbed along the tracks into the mountains and the night air grew cooler as they rose to the famous White Pass. Jim knew they must be near the Alaska border. His suspicion was soon confirmed. The truck stopped.

"Grab the stuff," instructed Roberts. "Two people on this morning's train from Skagway will pick it up. They're traveling on the cruise ship. Use the first garbage bin for the birds. The rest goes in the bathroom as usual. Don't mix them up. I'll stay with the truck."

Bongo extracted several packages from the cooler and headed into the night. As his footsteps faded up the tracks, the boys realized Bongo would travel the last leg on foot, thus avoiding taking the truck across the border into Alaska. He'd hide the packages where the tourist train ended its daily run and the accomplices would smuggle them to Skagway. When the tourists rejoined the cruise ship, they were home free. It was a slick operation.

In the silence of the cool night, the boys prayed they wouldn't be discovered. The hydraulic mechanism went into action as Roberts lowered the truck to the ground, drove off the tracks and turned back toward Bennett Lake. He then repositioned the truck astride the tracks and threw the hydraulics into action again, lifting the tires from the ground, ready for the return journey.

Just before the operation was complete, Matthew

remembered the cap door. He slithered along the floor and made sure the door was shut tight. Bongo returned, checked the door, and rejoined his partner.

8

SLEEP

By four-thirty in the morning the truck was approaching the campsite on Bennett Lake. Bongo had taken over the driving and Roberts had dozed off, influenced, no doubt, by his steady intake of alcohol.

"Hey, Roberts," said Bongo, shaking his partner awake. "Are we gonna stop and check on those kids again? We're almost at the camp."

"The kids?" asked Roberts, still in a daze. "What kids? Oh, yeah...the kids. Nah, they're harmless. Let's just get back to Carcross and get off these tracks."

Matthew and Jim struggled to stay awake. They were exhausted. Now they had to make a quick decision. Could they jump from the moving truck safely?

"Dad always says not to make important decisions when you're tired," drawled Matthew. He could barely keep his eyes open.

Jim tried to think it through, but his mind wouldn't cooperate. He kept seeing an image of Ashley and Jonathan worrying about Matthew. "We'd better get out while the getting's good," he said.

"But the getting *isn't* good," replied Matthew.

Jim decided they had to jump. He crawled to the rear of the truck. "When I get on the bumper," he whispered, "I'll help you out. Hold onto me and we'll jump together."

As soon as Matthew was out, Jim grabbed him tightly and jumped. Luckily, he hit the ground between the ties and rolled. He was surprised how easy it was.

"Radical," exclaimed Matthew. "We *did* it!"

"Stay down until they're out of sight," said Jim. "Let's not push our luck."

Minutes later they walked into camp. Matthew couldn't wait to tell their story. He knew Ashley and Jonathan would be worried, but he also knew he and Jim had cracked open the mystery of the bear killers.

There were embers in the fire, but the camp was empty. Ashley and Jonathan were nowhere to be found.

"They're looking for us," said Jim. "Probably at the underground lodge. Why does life have to be so complicated?"

Matthew found some beef jerky and put wood on the fire. "Not a problem," he said. "They'll be back soon. I can tell."

"Shouldn't we look for them?" asked Jim. "They'll be steamed at me for getting you in trouble."

"Getting me in trouble?" laughed Matthew. "Man, you're confused. You saved me. Besides, I'm not going near that place again. It's dangerous to my health." He paused, letting the tension drain from his body. "Do you realize I was in winter today...I mean yesterday? In some kind of season-warp with spooks I could see through? I've been in B.C. and nearly in Alaska. And I thought Los Angeles was weird."

Jim wasn't so relaxed. He enjoyed hanging with Matthew, Jonathan and Ashley. Things seemed to happen wherever they were. It was exciting, but he was afraid the twins would think he was unreliable. He paced nervously, oblivious to the sound of trout rising to the lake's surface for a morning meal.

"When we write the story about the ancient dwelling," said Matthew, "you should write the part about how you could smell the salt, how you felt connected to the place, but not connected at the same time. It's as if you have memories from before you were born. That way, we'll have different views, know what I mean? I can hardly wait to send it to the newspapers."

"Geez, Matthew, don't you ever stop thinking? Give me a break."

Matthew looked at Jim questioningly. "What am I supposed to do? *Not* think?"

The grass at the edge of the camp rustled and Jonathan and Ashley appeared. "You'd better think fast,

Matthew Adams," said Ashley. "And it better be a good story."

Matthew tried to look casual. "Chill, Ash. It's a *great* story. I'm sorry we messed up, but..."

Jonathan interrupted as he slumped by the fire. "Now I understand why parents get uptight sometimes. We figured those spirits grabbed you guys. We didn't know what to do. So we hung around in case you popped up out of nowhere. We couldn't figure it out. What happened? Are you all right? How did you get back here without us seeing you?"

Before the twins arrived, all Matthew could think about was telling them about the high railer. Now that they were back, he was too tired to talk. He tried to tell them about finding the truck on the tracks, but he was on empty. "Jim, you tell them," he said. "I can't stay awake. Good night everyone."

"Good *morning,* you mean," said Ashley, as Matthew stumbled to the tent.

"Maybe we all should get some sleep," said Jonathan. Ashley and Jim agreed. With the Yukon morning awaking, the campsite on Bennett Lake soon settled into a peaceful slumber.

BETRAYED?

By noon everyone was up and ready for whatever the day would bring.

"This is the best place in the world for summer," observed Matthew. "You wake up at lunch time and still have the whole day."

"Yeah, but in the winter we only get five or six hours of daylight," said Jim. "That can be tough."

"We have to decide what to do," said Jonathan. "After what you heard, we have to tell the police. There's nothing more we can do on our own."

"If we tell the cops in Carcross," said Jim, "they probably won't believe us."

"How can they not believe us?" asked Ashley. "All they have to do is find the truck. That should be easy."

Jim shook his head. "That's not how things work," he said. "Believe me. You can't arrest them for having a truck with train wheels on it. If you catch them on the tracks, maybe they can be charged with trespassing. The falcons and gall bladders are already gone, probably halfway to Taiwan by now. If the cops want to do anything, they have to get cooperation from British Columbia and Alaskan authorities."

The twins knew what Jim said was true. "Dad says the justice system often isn't about justice anymore, it's mainly about laws," said Ashley. "It's like if everyone tries to stick just to the written rules, fairness gets ignored. But he also says justice has always been complicated, even when it looked simple."

"I have a simple solution," said Matthew. "We call Mr. Priest. He can tell us what to do. He can tell the R.C.M.P. those guys shot at us. They'll believe him."

"Sounds like a good idea," said Ashley.

"Who is Mr. Priest?" asked Jim.

"Dad's friend," replied Jonathan. "He lives on Marsh Lake. He took us to Bove Island."

"He's retired and he's really nice," said Ashley.

Matthew was relieved when Mr. Priest answered the phone. He explained where they were and what had happened.

"Is your boat OK?" asked Stew.

"Sure," replied Matthew.

"Here's what we'll do. You head back to Carcross. I'll meet you with the truck on the sandy beach at the north end of the lake. Then we'll make a report to the R.C.M.P., how's that?"

"All right," said Matthew. "We'll leave in about half an hour."

"OK," said Stew. "Be careful in that boat."

"I'm glad that's settled," said Ashley. "It's a good move to get out of here."

Soon the fire was doused, everything was packed, and they headed up Bennett Lake toward Carcross. The water was calm, with a soft breeze occasionally slipping across the surface. They spotted a loon and Matthew guided the boat into a cove and stopped the motors. They watched as the big bird disappeared beneath the surface and reappeared some distance away. Ashley noticed that the loon was becoming Matthew's favorite animal.

They eventually caught sight of the end of the lake. Jim pointed to the long, sandy beach where they would meet Mr. Priest. Matthew aimed the boat toward shore. Mr. Priest should have been there by now, but there was no one to be seen.

Out of nowhere the roar of a powerful engine suddenly bore down on them with startling speed. They turned to see a bright aluminum jet boat coming right at them.

"What's he doing?" yelled Ashley. "He's coming right at us...he's going to ram us!"

At the last possible instant the jet boat sliced away, missing them by a few feet. The waves from the larger craft sent their boat bobbing crazily, forcing them to hang on for their lives. Then they saw Roberts at the wheel. Bongo stood grinning at his side.

"Gun the motors, Matthew," yelled Jonathan. "We have to get to shore!" Matthew opened up the twin five-horse motors, but their speed was pathetic compared to the jet boat's.

"Here he comes again," shouted Ashley. She grabbed the rifle. If these smugglers were going to threaten them, she figured, they were going to pay a price.

"No!" yelled Jim. "Put the gun down. It'll just make them mad. They aren't going to ram the boat."

Ashley hesitated. She and her brothers had been taught since they were young to look after themselves, to defend themselves. They were being threatened by smugglers

79

and Jim was telling her to put the rifle down. She was torn between two actions.

"Put it down," repeated Jim, his voice quiet in the midst of the screaming engines. Ashley put the rifle down, her eyes telling Jim it was an act of trust she didn't take lightly. Jim held her gaze. He knew what she was thinking. Without speaking, his eyes answered that he *knew* he was right.

The jet boat was on them again. Suddenly, Roberts cut the engines and pulled alongside. Bongo stood menacingly, cradling his .416—the elephant gun.

"Ahoy, maties. Har, har, har," laughed Roberts. "Shut down yer engines. Me name's Black Bob, but I ain't here to rob. Say yer prayers, maties. Yer through meddlin' in other people's business."

"Go pick on someone your own size and leave us alone," yelled Matthew.

"Shut your face, you little rat," sneered Roberts. "I have some special treats in store for you. Things I learned in 'Nam. Pull up your motors and get in here. Bongo, tie them up and secure that rinky dink raft."

Within minutes they were headed south. The jet boat barely touched the water as it took a course down the center of the lake. Jonathan caught Ashley's attention and nodded toward the beach where Mr. Priest was supposed to meet them. The beach was still empty.

THE CHURCH

In practically no time they were flying past the spot where their camp had been. The jet boat skimmed the blue water's surface. It wasn't long before Jim saw the cutline through the trees on both sides of the lake, indicating they were crossing into northern British Columbia.

Jonathan and Ashley were worried. What had begun as excitement had degenerated into something sinister. Roberts and Bongo were clearly serious. They were outsiders who were in the Yukon only as part of a smuggling ring with international connections. For some reason the men thought the four posed a threat. Apparently they weren't prepared to let anything, or anyone, interfere with their plans.

Matthew was perplexed. He couldn't figure out what had happened. The jet boat had intercepted them just as they were about to meet Mr. Priest. It was as if they expected the meeting at the beach. Roberts and Bongo didn't know they had been seen dumping the bear carcasses or driving to the Alaskan border. It didn't add up.

Roberts swung to the right and throttled back the motor. The boat ran up on the sandy shore's edge without protest. They had reached the southern end of Bennett Lake.

"End of the line, you little bozos. We're going for a walk. Don't give us trouble or you won't live to see another sunset. Bongo, tie up the boat and walk behind them."

81

Roberts led them from the lake's edge up a gentle slope. There were few trees but wildflowers were everywhere. Ashley was always amazed at the beauty of the Northern flowers. She thought the butterflies floating merrily along must be happy to have this secret place for their private use.

No one spoke. It soon became clear Roberts was leading them to some old, abandoned buildings nearby. Ashley guessed this must be the ghost town called Bennett that Jim had mentioned.

"Where are you taking us?" she asked. "What's your problem, anyway? We haven't done anything to you." Roberts frightened her. He seemed to have a real attitude. She had the unpleasant feeling that he was a dangerous man.

Roberts ignored her and kept walking. They passed near the old buildings, each of which had completely fallen apart. They seemed to be heading toward what was left of the largest building, which was located on a rise above the rest.

Drawing closer, they saw the building had once been a church. The timbers still standing suggested it had been an imposing structure. Roberts stopped at a doorway beneath where the steeple once stood and waved them through. For a brief moment, it seemed almost funny.

They were being ushered into a church with no doors and no roof.

"We should blindfold them," suggested Bongo.

"There's no point," replied Roberts. "They already know too much. Give me a hand with this."

They watched as the two men removed several loose floorboards. To their amazement, there was a stone slab hidden where a dirt floor should have been. Bongo grasped a metal ring embedded in the stone and pulled with all his considerable strength. The slab rose slowly, revealing stone steps leading down into the Yukon earth. Ashley cringed.

"In you go, maties," ordered Roberts. "You'll love our little hideaway." He roughly shoved Jonathan into the blackness. He tried to push Ashley, but Jim quickly inserted himself between her and Roberts. Ashley started down the steps on her own.

"Such a cute girl," sneered Roberts. "Too bad those good looks and blond hair will be wasted." A shiver ran down Jim's spine. He recognized the feeling of hatred the man radiated, but he didn't know where he had seen it before.

Matthew noticed, too. He was frightened. In spite of his fear, he caught Bongo's eye. "Your friend's a sicko, Bongo. You better watch your back."

Roberts grabbed him roughly and almost threw him down the steps. "I'm warning you for the last time, little guy, shut your mouth. C'mon, Bongo, we've gotta figure out what to do with them." His flashlight steady, Roberts descended the stairs. Bongo followed, pulling the stone slab shut behind him.

9

KUSAWA

The stairs led to a series of small, dark rooms with doorways, but no doors. The walls and ceilings were not reinforced with timbers, yet the rooms were perfectly preserved. Bongo put Ashley and Matthew back to back and tied their hands together. He did the same with Jim and Jonathan. Then he tied their feet and pushed the four to the floor in a room that looked like a cell.

"Try anything funny and you're dust," said Roberts. He and Bongo went to a nearby room. The children could hear them talking but couldn't make out their words.

"We've done it this time," said Jonathan, speaking into the darkness. "Who'd believe this?"

"I wonder what these rooms were for?" asked Matthew.

"The walls are just bare earth."

"Maybe storerooms," said Jim. "But the entrance is too well hidden to have been just a place to store things."

"Well, we know what they're for now," said Ashley. "It's a hideout. We have to find a way to escape. That Roberts guy scares me."

"What I can't figure out," said Matthew, "is how they knew we were going to meet Mr. Priest? How did they know where we were going to meet him? I mean, they were right there."

"That's right," said Jonathan. "When you think about it, how did they know where to cut us off? Maybe Mr. Priest told them where he was supposed to meet us. Besides, Roberts said we knew too much. How could he know we knew anything if someone hadn't told him? They didn't know what Jim and Matt saw."

Their conversation was broken by new sounds coming from the adjoining room. The voices were suddenly louder. Roberts and Bongo were talking to someone else.

Then they heard the rapid *tap tap tap* of something moving in their room. The sound was near floor level. They couldn't see anything, but they could hear a panting noise and the tapping sound moving about the room. No one dared breathe.

Then Ashley screamed. She jerked herself backward along the floor, ramming Matthew into the wall. She screamed again.

"It's trying to bite my face!" A cold, clammy tongue swiped across her cheek. "It's biting my face! Jonathan, help me...help!"

Her screams brought Roberts running with his flashlight. "What the hell's going on?" he yelled. "What the...?" He stopped short. "Oh my," he said sarcastically. "The little girlie is being attacked by the big, bad puppy dog. You kids are one giant pain, you know that?"

Roberts was joined by Bongo and a third man. The man was tiny, less than five feet tall. He wore a dark trench coat and a hat pulled over his forehead. He stood quietly in the background, saying nothing—but watching.

With the light from the flashlights, Ashley saw what had been attacking her. It was a young dog, now quivering beside the third man, tongue dangling from its mouth. The dog was more frightened than Ashley. Her fear left instantly, replaced by the shock of the familiar.

The puppy had obviously licked her face because they were friends. Standing at the feet of the mysterious third man was Mr. Priest's Labrador retriever, Kusawa. Ashley almost called the dog's name, stopping just before it tumbled from her lips. She looked at Jonathan and knew he recognized Kusawa, too.

The men laughed as they returned to their room. The tiny man dragged Kusawa away by his collar.

"That little guy is the same one I saw with Roberts and Bongo before," said Jim. "Did you notice? He never says a word and always hangs back. I'll bet he's the one called Wing."

"Man, this is getting stranger all the time," said Jonathan. "That was Mr. Priest's dog, Kusawa. What's

Kusawa doing here with Wing?"

"Mr. Trench Coat," said Matthew. "Mr. Solid Dresser."

"Be serious, Matthew," said Ashley. "This isn't funny."

"OK, I'm serious," said Matthew. "The problem is, I don't think there's any way we can untie these ropes."

"There's a way," insisted Ashley. "We just have to figure it out." As she wriggled her hands, she felt something in Matthew's back pocket. "Matthew, what's in your pocket?"

"My pocket?" asked Matthew. In a flash he remembered. "The scraper...Bongo missed the Tagish scraper."

"Let's see if we can get it," said Ashley, her voice quiet. "Maybe we can cut the ropes with it."

Matthew hesitated. He remembered how his visit with the Ahlonē seemed to be linked to rubbing the ancient scraper. When he told the others his story, he didn't mention that. Now he didn't know what to do. "Uh...Ash, there's a minor problem with the scraper," he said. "See, I think when you rub it...Ashley, get your hands off the scraper!"

It was too late. Ashley grabbed the scraper. With their hands tied together, it was difficult to hold. She fumbled it a bit. That's all it took.

A stiff breeze swept the room, as though someone had thrown open a window. The breeze became a gale and Matthew felt himself being swept from the floor and twirled in midair. In the darkness he could see nothing, but in his mind's eye he saw Ashley's image. He shouted her name. "Ashley! Help!"

THE AHLONĚ, II

The wind stopped. Matthew could still hear the echo of his plea for help. He opened his eyes slowly, afraid to see what he knew would be there. He was already chilled from the cold.

He was outside the old church, hands and feet untied. His first instinct was to run, but where would he go? He shivered. Then he noticed it wasn't cold. It wasn't winter...it was warm.

"It's not winter," he exclaimed. "At least it's not winter."

"How observant," said a voice behind him. "I'm glad you're comfortable."

Matthew turned to face his sister. "Ash...they took you, too! Ash, I'm sorry about the scraper...I should have told you. Only..."

"Stop worrying, Matthew. It's not your fault." She looked around. "It's springtime," she said, pointing to the lake. "Look, there's still ice on Bennett Lake."

"Yeah," said Matthew. "I can smell it. It smells like spring."

"What happens now? Do the ghosts, or whatever, come and get us?" she asked.

"I don't know," said Matthew. "But I know one thing. If we rub the scraper again, we might get back to..." He hesitated, realizing how ridiculous their situation was.

"Right," said his sister, "we might get back to Bongo and Roberts."

"Geez, Ash, what are we going to do?"

"Over here," came a high-pitched voice from within the church walls. "Come over here."

Ashley and Matthew looked at each other, bewildered.

"Over here," the voice repeated. "Come over here. We will not hurt you."

They saw a tiny figure peek from behind a fallen roof timber. He was no more than two feet tall and wore a loose-fitting brown garment belted around his waist. He waved for them to come into the ruins.

"He doesn't look scary," said Ashley. "I guess we should do what he says."

"Yeah," said Matthew, "but wait until he turns into a big white shape, waves his arms and makes it winter. Then he'll look scary."

"Come on, Matt, let's get it over with." She entered the church.

Several more tiny figures appeared as Ashley and Matthew approached. Ashley hesitated, then decided she had no choice.

"Hi. My name's Ashley Adams and this is my brother..."

"This is your brother Matthew Adams," said the apparent leader. "We are happy to meet you."

"Who are you?" asked Matthew. "Are you ghosts, or what? Did you bring us here?"

"So many questions, so many questions," came the response. "We are the Ahlonē people. You can think of us as spirits, if you wish." The tiny man grinned playfully and his eyes sparkled like the sun reflecting in a snowflake. "But, to be honest, we think of *you* as the spirits."

"Wait a minute," said Matthew. "The other ones, the big white guys I could see through...they said they were the Ahlonē people, too."

This brought the tiny figures to life. They all spoke at once, their high-pitched voices filling the air. The leader calmed them down.

"They say they are Ahlonē, but they are not," he said. "They are the Others, the outcasts, the fearful. They are not Ahlonē. We are the Ahlonē people, we are the Wind. By the way, the Others are not as big as you think, Matthew. They are masters of deception. They are the same as us, but they wish to appear bigger. So they deceive themselves by pretending to be bigger than they really are. Now, please come with us, you must meet someone."

With that, the little people left the church and headed away from the lake into the bush. Matthew and Ashley followed. Moving toward the foothills, the Ahlonē had a happy-go-lucky air about them. Matthew thought they seemed a cheerful bunch of spirit-things. Ashley thought so, too, especially after seeing how some scampered along, bright smiles lighting their faces.

They soon came to a wide, shallow river. It was shallow for Matthew and Ashley, that is, but would have been very deep for the Ahlonē.

"Where are we going?" asked Ashley, standing at the river's edge. "Do we cross the river?"

"We are going there," said the leader. He pointed to a cliff on the opposite side of the river. The rocky cliff rose hundreds of feet straight up from the river's edge. Ashley could see many small openings in its face and wondered if the Ahlonē lived there.

"But how are we going to get up there?" asked Matthew. "It's sheer rock."

The leader held out his hands. "Little tiny fingers, Matthew, fit little tiny cracks. We can climb that wall in no time. You and Ashley, on the other hand, could have a problem."

"All we seem to have are problems," sighed Ashley. "Does it ever end?"

"Perhaps," said one of the Ahlonē, "you would like the caribou to come to you?"

"The caribou?" asked Ashley. "What do caribou have to do with....oh, I get it. You're asking spirit questions only you know the answers to, right? Tell me, can other people see you, or just us?"

"You will know soon...*if* you can climb the cliff."

"C'mon, Ash," said Matthew. "We can climb the wall in the gym. We can handle it."

"I suppose we have no choice. Let's go, then. Anyone want a ride across the river?" She started into the gentle current.

10

PRINCESS LEOLIN

The next thing they knew they were standing in an opening halfway up the cliff. Their shoes weren't even wet.

"Awesome," breathed Matthew, looking at the endless drop to the river below. "How do you do that?"

"Follow me," instructed their guide. "Watch your heads. This place is not made for big people."

Matthew grinned and nudged his sister. "Hear that, Ash? We're the big people for a change." He threw back his shoulders and straightened up—only to bump his head on the ceiling. "Ow!" he yelped.

Moments later they entered a large room. A tiny Ahlonē woman sat in a chair surrounded by caribou skins. The chair was on an elevated platform of flat stones. Her short black hair glimmered in the soft cavern light. She stood and greeted her guests.

"Welcome, Ashley and Matthew Adams. I am Leolin, Princess of the Ahlonē people."

Matthew and Ashley looked at the beautiful woman standing before them. She seemed to glow.

"Hello, Princess Leolin," said Ashley. "Are you the leader of the Ahlonē people?"

"Yes," she replied, taking her seat. "Everyone does what I say, but they do not have to. It is an informal arrangement."

"Do you have a king and queen, too?" asked Matthew. "Isn't it usually a king or queen who's the leader?"

"Matthew," said Ashley. "Excuse him, Princess Leolin, he gets carried away."

"I get carried away, all right," agreed Matthew. "Carried away by big white spirits, carried away by bear killers, carried away by little..."

"Poor Matthew," interrupted the Princess. "Life is so full of difficulties."

"Are you really the boss?" asked Matthew.

"Head honcho at your service," replied the Princess, smiling.

"Can other people see you," asked Ashley, "or just us?"

"Only a few children can see us," replied Princess Leolin. "Perhaps one every ten seasons. We do not get involved often."

"Can you make the seasons change like the big white

guys?" asked Matthew.

"No problem." She raised her hand as though to change the season, but Matthew stopped her.

"No...please don't make it winter," he pleaded. "Please!"

"All right, Matthew, I will not," she said, smiling mischievously.

"Who are the Ahlonē people?" asked Ashley. "This is very confusing."

"We are the Wind," said Leolin. "The South Wind. We are the independent people—the explorer, the artist, the crafter, the trader, the jester and the shaman. We are the people of ideas."

"And the Others?" asked Ashley. "Who are they?"

"The same. The only difference between us is that they are unhappy, while we are happy."

"Is everyone either one or the other?" asked Matthew. He was seriously confused.

"Of course not," she replied. "There are only a few of either of us. Since seasons began, some tribe members enjoyed thinking for themselves, doing things those who had gone before had not yet done. Some went too far and were banished from the tribe. We, and the Others, are those who were exiled."

"You mean you surfed off the edge?" asked Matthew.

"Exactly," confirmed the Princess.

"And everyone else?" asked Ashley. "What happens to them?"

Princess Leolin pointed upward. "They are there," she said, quietly. "When you see the Northern Lights, they are celebrating. We never get to celebrate with them. We would like to, but we do not worry about it. The Others, on the other hand...well, you might say they are permanently angry they are not able to party with the rest."

"Are you all Tagish Indians?" asked Matthew.

The tiny woman laughed. "No. We are all people. We are Tagish, Tlingit, Tutchone, Ahtna, Yup'ik, Inuit... everyone. The animals, too."

"Why are we here?" asked Ashley. "We know it has something to do with the scraper Matthew found, but there must be a reason."

"Yeah," said Matthew, "you've been really nice to us and everything, but I don't know what Dad will say. He's not going to let us go anywhere after this."

"If there is an after this," Ashley said to Matthew. "Don't forget, there's still Roberts and Bongo to deal with. And Mr. Priest, too."

"What happens now?" asked Matthew. "Are we wind spirits? Can you help us get away from those men so we can go to the police? Do you know anything about the ancient underground dwelling we found? Was it really built on the Alaskan coast?"

Everything Matthew said made the Princess smile. "There you go again, Matthew, asking questions. That is why the Others were angry with you—for asking too many questions. Did you figure it out? They do not like people asking questions. If you ask too many questions, they say you are trespassing."

Matthew's eyes widened. He'd never heard such a

thing. How could people not ask questions?

"What happens now?" asked Ashley. "What about the scraper?"

Princess Leolin sighed. Ashley could see she wasn't comfortable with the subject. "Yes, of course...the scraper. The problem is that Matthew was not supposed to find it. Jim was."

"Jim?" asked Matthew. "You mean you put it there for Jim to find? Why?"

"It is complicated. You see, there is a contest, and it is about Jim. He was supposed to find the ancient scraper and, through it, we had a chance to influence him. But you found it instead, Matthew, then you rubbed it and things went off track."

"What sort of contest?" asked Ashley.

"A contest for Jim's future. When he left home and went to Bove Island, the Others started working on him. They want him to be an Other. They stole his supplies, blew his boat away...things like that. We tried to stop them from interfering. We returned his things and put the scraper where we thought he would find it. You must realize that this is how things have been done since seasons began." Princess Leolin paused.

"You see, if the Others bother Jim so much that he begins to hate everything, then they will eventually win his future seasons. Later, he will become an Other, an unhappy outsider. We want to prevent that."

Matthew carefully removed the ancient scraper from his pocket. "I guess you want this back, huh?"

"Yes, please. I am afraid we must start again. But keep it until you rub it and return to the church at Bennett Lake."

"If we go back, we'll be tied up again by Roberts and Bongo," said Ashley.

"Do not worry," Leolin assured her, "we will help you get away from the church once you are back. But you will be on your own after that. We try not to interfere in people's affairs."

"Wow. This is fun again!" said Matthew, his confidence returning. "What's your plan for us to get away?"

"We will move some things around to distract Roberts and Bongo. That is all we can do in your world...move things. You should be able to escape in your boat. I am sure you will think of something." Her voice seemed to hold a challenge.

"Wait a minute," exclaimed Matthew. "It was you who moved our stuff, wasn't it? You put the communicator under Ashley's sleeping bag, right?"

Leolin smiled. "Yes, Matthew. We did it. But we were putting your things back. The Others took them, trying to frighten you away. We put them back, but we did not know where they had been taken from. So we just put them under Ashley's sleeping bag. We also frightened the Others away when they were about to sentence you, Matthew. They fear us."

"Should I rub the scraper now?" asked Matthew eagerly. "I can't wait to see what you do to those guys."

"There is only one problem," said Leolin. "Your

communicator. We will have to destroy it. Somehow you captured a part of us in it. I do not know how. This is the first time it has happened." For the first time her face showed a sign of sadness. "We do not like to destroy things because it is not our way. But we have no choice."

"Whoa," said Matthew. "Not the communicator...please! It's not even ours. It's just a loaner. We can work this out..." Suddenly he understood. "Are you talking about the noises I recorded? The high-frequency sounds only Ashley could hear? Is that it? I'm right, right?"

"Yes. Those noises are us talking...as we sound in your world. You have captured our thoughts and they must be set free."

Matthew relaxed. "No problem, Princess. I'll just erase them. You don't need to wreck the communicator."

"Erase them? You mean you can set them free?" She looked to Ashley for confirmation. "Can you do this?"

"Yes. We'll erase them. Guaranteed. You don't need to worry."

"Excellent." Princess Leolin seemed satisfied. "In that case, you should return to the church. Ashley, hold onto Matthew or you will be trapped here. Are you ready?"

"It's been fun talking to you," said Matthew. "I wish you were bigger and could meet my Dad. You would really get along. Don't you think so, Ash?"

Ashley stared at her little brother. "You're embarrassing sometimes, you know that? Rub the scraper before I leave without you."

She looked back to apologize to Princess Leolin, but

she was gone. Ashley and Matthew stood alone in an empty cliffside cave. She held Matthew's hands while he rubbed the scraper. The wind came from nowhere and again lifted them into the air. They were spun around and around, like on a ride at the circus. Ashley closed her eyes and held on for all she was worth.

11

CHOPPER!

As swiftly as it began, it ended. Ashley's first hint that they were back in the church came from a pair of strong hands gripping her shoulders.

"Ashley. Ashley," Jonathan whispered urgently. "Can you hear me? Are you all right?"

Ashley's eyes focused slowly. She could see Jim and Matthew standing above her. Jonathan was closer, but he looked fuzzy.

"I'm OK," she managed, though she wasn't sure it was true. "How did Matthew get here before me? Who untied your hands? What's happening?"

"You came back with Matthew, but you've been in a daze. Matt untied us and found a flashlight. We're ready to take off if you're all right. Can you walk?"

Ashley's mind was clearing fast. She heard the urgent tone of her twin brother's voice and pushed herself to her feet. "I'm ready," she said. "Can we get out?"

"Princess Leolin must be doing her thing," said Matthew. "The turkeys are running around cursing. We'd better move it." He went to the doorway, peeked around the corner, then waved the others forward.

Jim and Jonathan hit the stairs first. They hoped they could lift the stone slab together. To their relief, it rose on the first try and the four sprinted into the daylight. One after the other they tripped across debris lying on the abandoned church floor. In their haste to escape, they forgot their eyes needed time to adjust to the sunlight. For several seconds they couldn't see a thing.

One by one they picked themselves up. Matthew had added another nasty scrape to his leg to match the one from his spill on the railway track.

"The lake," yelled Jonathan, urging the others on. "We have to get to the lake. Run, Matthew, run!"

With the speed only terror can provide, they tore through the ghost town, racing for the lake's edge. The fact that they couldn't see Roberts, Bongo and Wing somehow made them even more frightened.

Jim reached the shore first. Their boat remained lashed to the jet boat. Jim untied the jet boat and together they pushed it into the water. An onlooker would have thought the four had practiced the routine a hundred times. Not a word was said, but within seconds they were all on board and zipping up their float coats.

Jim took the wheel and turned the key. The motor roared to life.

"Yahoo!" exclaimed Matthew. "We *did* it...we *did* it!"

Jim opened up the throttle and the boat spurted forward. He'd never had this much power at his fingertips. He glanced back, grinning with an exhilaration he felt to his toes. The grin vanished, however, when he saw Ashley, Jonathan and Matthew sprawled on the floor. He realized he'd taken off with a jolt—but he was the only one who was hanging on to anything!

Jim thought they might be upset, but when the shock cleared from their faces, the three started laughing.

"Welcome to the Yukon 500," said Jonathan. "Man, can this thing fly, or what?"

"All right!" squealed Matthew. "They'll never catch us now. Carcross, here we come."

The early evening air was warm on their faces as they flashed along the lake's surface. Bennett Lake was flat calm and the surrounding mountains reflected perfectly in the blue water. Ashley and Jonathan caught each other gazing at the hyper-colored scenery. They had gone from panic to serenity inside ten minutes. They smiled, knowing how lucky they were.

Jonathan noticed something in the boat. "Am I dreaming, or is that the communicator?" he asked.

Then Ashley and Matthew noticed, too.

"All our gear is here!" said Ashley. "They put everything in the boat!" She threw her head back and shouted toward the top of the mountains. "Thank you, Princess Leolin, wherever you are...thank you!"

"Princess Leolin?" asked Jonathan, a bewildered look on his face. "Are we talking head injury here?"

Ashley swiped the blond hair from her face. "Princess Leolin, dear brother, just came through for us. Right, Matthew?"

"Yup," he replied, grinning. It was fun knowing something his older brother didn't know for a change. "Jonathan, you should have seen her. Très Hollywood, believe me."

That proved to be the extent of their celebration. Though Jim was driving, he kept an eye out behind them in case anything unexpected occurred. Something unexpected *did* occur.

"Check it out," yelled Jim, pointing behind them. "What do you see?"

They looked back. There was a dot flying low in the blue sky—heading in their direction.

Ashley lifted the binoculars, her heart pumping wildly. "It's a chopper," she exclaimed. "I think it's heading toward us. Who could it be...the R.C.M.P.?"

"No," answered Jim. "It's not the right color. I don't know who it is. Maybe geologists."

The helicopter was drawing closer. Ashley had the binoculars glued to her eyes. "Oh, no...we must not be living right. It's Wing. It's the trenchcoat with his droids!" Then she caught on to what was happening. "Jim," she yelled, "watch out! He's aiming that big rifle at us. Jim!"

The crack of the rifle could be heard even over the screaming helicopter and jet boat engines. Jim heaved the

steering wheel sharply to the right and everyone again lost their balance. The shot missed.

The chopper came closer, but Jim wove the boat back and forth too quickly for Bongo to get a good shot. It was clear Wing had no intention of letting them get away. Handling the helicopter like a stunt pilot, he swung around in front of the boat, hovering not ten feet above the lake's surface.

"He's forcing us to shore," yelled Jim. "I can't keep dodging him."

Matthew glanced at the shore. He saw the familiar beach where they had camped the night before. "Jim...run it up on the beach. I know where we can hide."

Jim wasn't sure what to do. It was fun driving the boat when they escaped, but he didn't like the feeling he had right now. If he did the wrong thing, he'd be responsible. He checked with Ashley and then Jonathan. Their eyes told him they didn't have any better ideas. They shrugged.

"Hang on," yelled Jim, "we're going to crash-land!" He pointed the boat at the beach, which was coming up in a hurry. The move caught Wing by surprise and he looped the chopper around behind them.

Matthew obviously had a plan. As the others braced for the impact, he looked like he could hardly wait. "When we hit, follow me," he shouted. "If they land, I know where to hide. If they don't, we'll hide in the trees."

The words were barely out of his mouth when the jet boat slammed into the sand. Jim cut the motor just as they were about to hit, but the boat rode fifty feet across the sand anyway. It remained upright and the four shaken passengers quickly clambered over the side.

No one took the time to check where the helicopter was. If they had, they would have seen Wing hovering patiently several hundred feet from shore. He'd been certain the kids were bluffing. They weren't really going to beach the boat. He guessed wrong.

Matthew led the way into the trees. When they reached cover, they stopped to see what Wing would do next.

"If he lands, we go for the underground lodge," said Matthew, panting for breath. "If he stays up, we can't run. He could see us running through the trees."

"For sure," said Jim, "especially the way Wing flies that thing. He's a hot pilot."

"Matthew," said Ashley, still catching her breath, "what makes you think we can hide there? They'll see us go in. Even if they don't, remember they're professional trackers. They'll find us for sure."

"They're professional poachers," said Jim. "Without their chopper or airplane, I'll bet they couldn't follow a whole herd of caribou."

"Either way, we have a big problem," concluded Ashley.

Their thoughts were cut off by the heavy *whoop whoop whoop* of the approaching helicopter. Wing swung the machine back and forth as though trying to decide what to do. He didn't wait long. He set it down on the beach near the boat.

The children ran for their lives, staying in the trees as much as possible. Everyone prayed Matthew's plan would work. They were out of options. The hunters were closing in.

To their surprise, however, the helicopter blades didn't even slow down. Wing didn't land after all. He just touched down and took off immediately.

"He must have dropped Bongo off," Ashley yelled to the others. "Or maybe Roberts. What should we do?"

"Keep running!" urged Matthew. "We have to get to the lodge. Run!"

Wing watched the four stupid children run through the trees. They were tough, but nobody could interfere with Wing Toh and live to tell about it.

Roberts and Bongo were only a hundred yards behind when Matthew and the others scrambled into the hole in the ground. Wing smiled grimly and looked for a spot to land the chopper.

Once inside, Matthew gave the orders. "Follow me," he said, shining his flashlight ahead of him. He led them to a wall near the end of the lodge.

"Matthew," said Ashley, "I hope you know what you're doing. Wing saw us come in here, you know. I'm really

107

scared." Something about Matthew's calm attitude made her think that maybe, just *maybe,* he really had a plan.

"Right here," said Matthew. He stood near the wall where a line of large stones separated one living area from the next. The stones were piled about three feet high.

"C'mon, Matt," urged Jonathan, "what's the plan?"

"See anything?" asked Matthew.

"Please, Matthew," pleaded Ashley.

"I just want you to look, that's all," said Matthew. "That way, when we're inside, you won't worry."

They studied the wall carefully but could see nothing.

"What are we looking for?" asked Jim.

"OK," said Matthew, satisfied they weren't going to catch on. "Carefully move the stones next to the wall. We don't want to make a mess."

Jim and Jonathan removed the top stone. It took both of them to lift it. Then they saw what Matthew was talking about. Behind the stone was an opening carved into the wall. They removed another large stone. There was now enough room for Ashley to climb in. The hiding place was easily large enough for everyone.

"All right, genius," said Jonathan, "get in there." He was smiling broadly as his little brother clambered into the hole. "You next, Jim."

Once everyone was safely inside, Jonathan pulled the stones back in place. Wing and his hired guns weren't going to catch their prey today.

12

GRANDFATHER MO

They could hear Roberts and Bongo searching. A glint of light passed through a tiny crack where the stones met the wall. They huddled in the dark and prayed.

"There's no one here," Bongo said. "I'm getting a sore neck. This place is too small. I'll be outside."

"Don't be an idiot," said Roberts. "Wing saw them come in, so they're here. I can't wait to get my hands on them."

"You and Wing can look 'till hell freezes over, but I'm outta' here," said Bongo. "At least you two are the right size for this hole in the ground."

They shuffled off, no doubt uneasy about having to report their failure to the boss. Soon the silence was again broken by the sound of someone searching.

"Wing," whispered Ashley. Her body tensed. The sounds suggested Wing was searching more carefully than the others. The secret hiding place was well concealed, however, and Wing soon gave up.

After ten minutes of total silence, the four realized their hiding place was as much a trap as an escape. They had no way of knowing if their pursuers were waiting for them or if they were gone. The minutes seemed like hours. Finally, Ashley couldn't take it. "We can't sit here forever," she whispered. "We have to do something."

"You're right," agreed Jonathan, "but what? They're probably waiting outside. We're trapped."

"When I read how ancient people hid from enemies like this," said Matthew, "it seemed like a great idea. Now I'm not so sure. They should have built a tunnel to get outside."

"Maybe they did," said Jim. "Maybe this isn't the only hiding place. I'll bet there are others. If we could find them, it would be great for your story, Matthew."

Jonathan made a decision. He nudged the top stone away from the entrance. Then he nudged it a bit more. Soon there was enough room for Matthew to squeeze out.

"Matt," whispered Jonathan, "it's up to you...be careful."

Matthew slipped through the opening and tried to get oriented. On hands and knees he moved quietly toward the entrance. It was farther than he remembered.

Soon he returned and announced they could come out. "They're gone," he said, relief evident in his voice. "I don't see the chopper anywhere."

Outside, everyone was still nervous. They didn't know if someone was hiding nearby, waiting to pounce. But as the minutes slid by, it seemed more and more likely they were safe. They retrieved some gear from the big boat. Their inflatable was still tied to its side, but it was damaged beyond repair.

Carrying only essentials, they set out to follow the shore of Bennett Lake back to Carcross. It would be a long hike, but they agreed they had little choice. They were grateful there was no shortage of daylight.

The sun had settled behind the mountains when the four tired hikers crossed the bridge into Carcross. In the half darkness of the Yukon summer night, their single-file formation looked like weariness itself. Once across the bridge, they rested in front of the town's General Store.

"I can't take any more," yawned Matthew. "I can't keep my eyes open."

"At least we made it," said Ashley, sitting on the edge of the wooden sidewalk. "I wonder why the stars are so bright in the North? Feel how soft the night is...like a friendly night. It's how I would make every night if I were master of the universe."

"Never noticed before how quiet it is in town in the middle of the night," said Jim. "It's exceptional."

"Yeah," agreed Jonathan. "That's why we like camping here so much. Everywhere else it's bright lights and noise, heaters and coolers, motors, fans, televisions, computers, or radios. It never ends. Dad says it's the simpleness of camping that makes it so much fun."

"Who needs to be plugged in every minute?" asked Ashley.

"My Grandfather used to say the Tagish people lost a lot the day they put on a watch," mused Jim. "I think that's what he meant. Something like that, anyway." An idea suddenly occurred to him. "That's where we should go," he said, excitedly. "Let's go to my Grandfather's place."

"Right," yawned Matthew. "Hi, Grandpa. These are my friends from California. We're hiding from poachers who kidnapped us and we need a place to crash. Don't be upset it's the middle of the night, Grandpa. We'll be gone in the morning." He looked at his new friend. "I don't think so, Jim."

"I'm serious," insisted Jim. "He won't mind. He's always really relaxed. He just rolls with whatever happens."

"Jim," said Jonathan, throwing an arm around Jim's shoulder, "if you say we go to your Grandfather's house, we go to your Grandfather's house. Wherever we're going, we'd better go. I'm getting cold just sitting here."

With renewed energy, Jim led them along an unpaved road. "It's not far," he said. "I'm sure he won't mind." They soon approached an old log building with no light showing inside. Jim knocked softly and an old man opened the door.

Jim hesitated. What seemed like a great

idea only seconds ago suddenly seemed like a lousy idea. "Uh...hello, Grandfather. Uh...sorry to wake you up, but, ah...these are my friends from California and we're hiding from these poachers, and we don't have a place to go..." His voice trailed off.

Grandfather Mo smiled a smile of welcome. He loved visitors, even at three in the morning. "Come in, Jim, come in. Bring your friends. I'll make coffee." The man's every movement told them he was happy to see them, happy to have them in his home. He made it all feel so normal.

Soon a small fire was burning in the wood stove and the kettle was heating. The old man lit a lantern and made them comfortable. The house was essentially a kitchen space and a small sleeping room. There were only three old wooden chairs, so Jim and Jonathan sat on a trunk near the wall.

Jim's Grandfather looked about ninety years old, but in his eyes he was decades younger.

"Why not use the light, Grandfather?" asked Jim.

"It's summer, Jim. Don't use electricity if I don't have to. Besides, the lantern makes a better feeling. Are you going to introduce me to your friends?"

"Grandfather Mo, these are my friends Ashley, Jonathan and Matthew. They're from Palm Springs, California."

The old man shook their hands. Ashley noticed that his hands were soft. Everything about the man seemed soft. Even his voice was quiet.

"Is this a cabin from the olden days?" asked Matthew. He was fascinated by the tiny home. The logs inside were visible, just like in the cabins in ghost towns. Everything was clean and tidy, but even the small table looked ancient.

"Yes, Matthew, it's from Gold Rush times," Grandfather Mo replied. "As a matter of fact, it's a historic landmark. It's related to you, in a way."

"Me?" asked Matthew. "But I've never been here."

"The original owner was a famous Yukoner named Miss Matthews. There's a plaque on the front that says *Miss Matthews' Cabin*. So you're connected by your name. I should say that you look like a Yukon person, too."

Matthew liked the old man instantly. He knew he had just received a compliment.

"Hiding from poachers, are you? I was once a poacher, at least that's what they said. But it wasn't true. I only hunted as our people had always hunted. They fixed the laws since then. Now I'm a registered Indian. The only thing that changes is what the authorities decide to call me. But I stay the same." He looked at the others. "Forever, maybe." He laughed a quiet laugh. "Tell me your story."

They told him of their adventures. He listened intently, nodding his head occasionally, drinking coffee steadily. They were surprised that he seemed truly interested in what they were saying.

Grandfather Mo puffed his pipe. "I've seen some strange things in the Land of the Midnight Sun, but Stew Priest involved with poachers? I don't think so. Not his nature. By the way, he's been looking for you kids since yesterday. Has the R.C.M.P. searching. He's real worried."

"Maybe he's not involved," allowed Jonathan, "but I'm suspicious."

The old man looked at Jonathan and Ashley, as though scanning their characters. "Something's missing from your story," he said, finally. "You're only telling me part of it."

This statement brought Matthew back from the brink of sleep. He wanted more than anything to tell someone about the Ahlonē. He couldn't hold back any longer.

"If we say we saw a black truck with dead bears in it driving on abandoned railway tracks," he said, "do you think anyone will believe us? If we tell them we were kidnapped, tied up and held in a secret place under a church in a ghost town, will they believe us? Not! If we say a helicopter chased us across Bennett Lake, what will they think? So how can we tell anyone we've been talking to spirits? Two different kinds of ghosts. Headline—*CALIFORNIA KIDS SURF CYBERSPACE!* Or maybe *SEXY SPIRIT SAVES SIBLINGS—NATIVE TEENAGER SUBJECT OF SPIRIT SKIRMISH!*"

Grandfather Mo's pipe was in his mouth, but he wasn't smoking. His eyes grew wide as Matthew spoke. The others saw he was more interested than ever in what they had to say. As Matthew finished his outburst, the old man smiled broadly, placing his hand on Matthew's shoulder.

"You're a lucky boy, Matthew. You have seen the little people. It's a long time since I heard that someone saw the little people. I'm right, eh? You saw the *Inukin?* The *Ijiraq?*" He slapped his knee gleefully. "We have many legends about the little people. Sometimes they steal our salmon, sometimes they tease us by hiding things while we are in the bush. Some are playful, some are not so nice. You have to tell me everything. Different tribes call them different names. The Inupiat call them *Inukin.* I always liked that name best. This is the best news I've heard since Jim was born...you have to stay and tell me everything."

Relief swept the room. Matthew, particularly, felt much better. "You believe us?" he asked.

"Why shouldn't I believe you?" asked the old man. "We must write everything down, so nothing is forgotten. But maybe before you tell me the whole story, we should sleep. You're tired, I can see. When you're old, you won't need much sleep. You must sleep to grow strong."

Matthew and the twins laid out their sleeping bags. Jim didn't know whether to drink coffee or go to sleep. He couldn't decide. As the others settled in, he realized he was somehow different after tonight. He was curious about what his Grandfather meant when he said it was the best news he'd heard *since Jim was born.* He never knew his Grandfather thought it was good news when he was born.

The sun was up and the long summer day well underway when sleep took over the cabin. Their bodies were exhausted and their minds peaceful. Jim had picked the perfect place in Carcross to visit that night.

13

WING

"**Y**ou kids sure know how to find the eye of a storm," said the R.C.M.P. officer. "We've sent out descriptions of the men and we'll bring them in for questioning. Now that I have all the information, we'll follow up right away." She glanced at her computer screen. "Our file shows Mr. Priest reported shots fired at his boat on Marsh Lake. That was on your way to Bove Island, right?"

"Did he report the bear we found floating in the water?" asked Ashley.

The young officer scrolled through the file. "Nothing here about a bear. What happened?"

Ashley, Jonathan and Matthew exchanged glances.

"Well," began Ashley, "we think the reason those men were shooting at us was because we found a dead black bear floating in Marsh Lake. Mr. Priest said he'd report it. Maybe he forgot."

"Maybe he reported it to the Wildlife Department," suggested Jonathan. "Isn't it more their concern?"

The police officer shook her head. "Not really. Poaching is a business these days and we've had big-time problems the past few years. Countries where people use wild animal parts for medicine won't back off. They want caribou horn, bear gallbladders and bear paws. The demand grows and the supply shrinks every year. Not to mention the falcons. It's a major police problem." She checked her computer calendar. "In fact, we have a conference next week with the British Columbia police and the Alaska State Troopers to see if we can get a handle on it."

"I don't know why Mr. Priest didn't report it," said Jonathan.

"You can ask him in a few minutes," said the officer. "We have a message that he's coming to pick you up. He should be here soon."

They answered a few more questions and chatted with two other officers who wanted to meet them. Some details of their story had leaked out and people were curious to find out what was going on. Soon they wandered outside to wait for Mr. Priest.

"This is too weird," said Ashley. "We're worried that Mr. Priest is in with the poachers and he's the one who's picking us up. I'm not sure we should go with him."

"Yeah," agreed Jonathan. "It is weird. But I don't think he'd do anything—not after we've made a police report. We should be fine."

"What are you going to do now, Jim?" asked Ashley.

"I guess I'll...heck, I don't know. Maybe I should see if I can stay with my Grandfather for a while. My Dad doesn't seem to want me around."

"Hey," said Matthew, "why don't you come with us? It would be fun. Mr. Priest has lots of room at his cabin. I bet he wouldn't mind. We'll be here for two more weeks. You can show us the good fishing spots and we could write the story about the lodge. You could meet our father, too."

"Why not?" said Jonathan. "We can ask Mr. Priest."

Jim relaxed visibly and glanced at Ashley. That's when Matthew noticed something for the first time. He felt stupid he hadn't noticed it before. Jim had a crush on Ashley! Matthew smiled to himself. Jim better be careful—Ashley was always making friends, but not boyfriends.

Stew Priest finally showed up in his truck and they headed back to Marsh Lake. There was no problem with Jim coming along. After stopping by Grandfather Mo's house, they went to the medical clinic to have the nurse check Matthew's scrapes. Mrs. Priest met them when they arrived at the cabin.

"It's good to see you kids are all right," said Trudy Priest. "You had us on pins and needles." She gave each a big hug and was introduced to Jim. "Found a new friend, eh? C'mon in. I have moose sausage and ptarmigan all laid out. Fresh cranberry bread baked specially for you kids. Let's eat."

They recounted their adventures, still not letting on they suspected Stew had given them away. He said he went to the beach as planned, but they didn't show up.

"This bread is fantastic!" said Jim, eating his fourth slice.

"Jim," began Mrs. Priest, "I'm retired, so I have all day to make bread. Your parents probably have too much to do. You can't expect everyone to be able to slave over a hot oven all day kneading bread dough, getting tired out just to bake you bread. Right?"

Ashley, Jonathan and Matthew burst out laughing. Jim didn't see what was funny. He wondered what the joke was. He tried to put the bread back on his plate without anyone noticing. Maybe he had eaten too much.

"Ho, ho, ho, Mrs. Priest," giggled Matthew. "Don't listen to her, Jim. She loves to brag about how she slaves over a hot oven all day baking bread." He pointed to the counter. *"That's* what slaves all day. Mrs. Priest has two of them."

Trudy Priest laughed, too, and slapped Jim on the back. "I work *sooo* hard baking that bread."

"You should buy another bread maker and open a store," suggested Ashley.

"Yeah, and Mr. Priest could pinch the bread to feed the bluejays and ducks," laughed Matthew.

"Best fed birds in the whole Territory, right here at

Marsh Lake," said Stew. "My contribution to preserving wildlife."

"Except they aren't exactly wild anymore, Mr. Priest," said Matthew.

"What's that noise?" asked Ashley, cocking her head. "I hear a crackling sound."

"It's that scanner," replied Trudy. "Mary has it on all the time. I don't know why she listens to it and I don't know why she leaves it on when she goes out."

"Who's Mary?" asked Ashley.

"Oh, my heavens," exclaimed Trudy. "You kids haven't met Mary. Every summer she rents the little guest cabin behind our place. We built it so our children could visit, but they never do. So we rent it to Mary in the summer. She comes and goes; here for a week and then gone for a few days. I forgot she was away when you arrived last week."

"What's a scanner?" asked Ashley. "Like to scan pictures into a computer? What I hear sounds more like a radio."

"It is like a radio," replied Stew. "It's a receiver that picks up all kinds of radio signals ordinary radios don't. You can hear pilots talking to the control tower, police calls, and ambulances. Lots of things. It's interesting, I suppose, but Mary takes it to extremes. She has it on all the time. I guess she's just nosy."

"Aren't they illegal?" asked Jonathan.

"Don't know," replied Stew. "They are in some places, I guess."

"A friend of mine in Palm Springs has one," said Matthew, reaching for another piece of sausage. "One day we were listening..." He stopped in mid-sentence.

"Are you all right?" asked Trudy. "Are you choking? Is there something wrong with the sausage?"

"What's wrong, Matt?" asked Jonathan. "What is it?"

"I know what happened," declared Matthew. "I figured it out. That's how they knew we were going to meet you at Bennett Lake, Mr. Priest. *They heard us on a scanner!*"

"Of course," agreed Ashley. "It makes sense. They had a scanner and heard Matthew talking to Mr. Priest when they made the arrangements. They picked up the signal from the communicator's cellular phone." Ashley looked like a giant load had been lifted from her shoulders.

"You're not saying Mary is..." began Mrs. Priest.

"Oh, no," Ashley reassured her. "It's just that we couldn't figure out how they knew where we'd be, that's all."

"It could have been Mary," said Jim.

"It could have been anyone," said Matthew. The neurons were flashing through his mind. He sensed he was close to figuring something out, but he was stuck.

"I don't suppose the thought ever crossed your minds that I might have tipped them off?" asked Stew quietly. The silence his question met gave him his answer. He was seriously insulted.

"Don't be mad at us, Mr. Priest," pleaded Matthew. "We had to think of everything we could."

Stew excused himself and stepped outside. Ashley and

Jonathan knew his pride and dignity were hurt. Ashley, his favorite, went outside to apologize for doubting him.

"Please don't be upset, Mr. Priest. You have to understand. We had to try to figure out what was going on. When we saw Kusawa with Wing..."

Stew stopped in his tracks. "Kusawa? What do you mean, Ashley? Where did you see Kusawa? The dog hasn't been anywhere. How could you have seen her?"

Now Ashley was confused. Was it possible that the puppy in the church wasn't Kusawa? She had been so sure. So had Jonathan and Matthew. "Are you sure Kusawa was here all the time?" she asked. "She licked my face when we were tied up in the church."

"So you thought I was involved with the poachers? I guess you had reason. I'm sad you thought I could do something like that. It's kind of insulting to an old Yukoner like me."

Ashley took Stew's arm. "I'm sorry. Let's go back inside and figure this out. We were certain it was Kusawa." She gently guided him back toward the cabin.

Inside, Matthew was explaining to Trudy how he and Jim were going to write an article about the ancient dwelling they had found. They would do more research by accessing library databases on archaeology. Then they'd write it just like a formal report and fax it to a professional journal. They might write about it in a more informal way and fax the story to major newspapers, too.

"But if you do that," said Trudy, "won't the site get overrun with journalists from Outside? They'd ruin it, wouldn't they?"

"We're not going to tell them exactly where it is," said Jim. "We'll just mention the general vicinity. Eventually, though, we'll tell a university—maybe one in Alaska or the Yukon. They can study it properly."

"Ashley warned you Matt would rope you into his project," said Jonathan. "Looks like she was right."

"Better than sitting alone on Bove Island wondering who I am," replied Jim, with a grin. Through the window he saw Ashley and Mr. Priest. As he watched, a car turned onto the road leading to the cabin. A figure stepped out and walked toward the cabin. Behind the figure Jim saw a puppy scampering playfully.

"It's Wing," he said, almost to himself. "It's *Wing!*"

The others joined him at the window. Sure enough, heading straight for them was a tiny figure in a dark trench coat.

"Oh my, you kids slay me," said Mrs. Priest. "That's not your infamous Mr. Wing, chopper pilot extraordinaire. That's just Mary...Mary Toh, the young woman who rents our guest cabin."

14

THE CHASE

Clouds slid across the blue sky, wrapping Marsh Lake in a dark twilight. Whitecaps suddenly dotted the lake's surface as though they were lying in wait for a chance to show their stuff. With each step Mary Toh took toward the cabin, the breeze rose a notch. Stew Priest looked skyward. Trees swayed back and forth and branches leaped as they were caught by wind gusts. A mean summer storm was rolling in.

As though responding to a sixth sense, Ashley glanced down the long, dusty laneway. She saw Mary Toh at the same instant Mary Toh saw her. A clap of thunder wiped out Ashley's words. *"It's Wing!"*

Jonathan, Matthew and Jim crashed through the door

heading for Wing. Wing, reacting equally fast, turned and sprinted for the lake. She was met by sheets of driving rain. Ashley stood frozen on the deck, transfixed by the thought that the mysterious Wing, the same Wing who had tried to run them into Bennett Lake with a helicopter, was a woman! For no reason Ashley understood, her temper flew off the scale.

Stew didn't know what was happening. He saw the boys fly out the door after Mary, saw Mary take off for the lake, and realized he, too, was running only after Ashley jerked him off the deck and down the steps. Trudy stood in the window wondering if there was anything she should bring in out of the rain.

Stew and Ashley soon caught up with Matthew, who couldn't keep pace with Jonathan and Jim. Stew was quickly running out of breath, but Ashley had such a tight grip on his arm he had no choice but to keep moving.

"What's going on?" Stew asked as they raced toward the dock.

The wind was blowing so hard Matthew barely heard the question. He pointed at their quarry. *"Wing!"* he yelled, "she's *Wing!"*

"She isn't Wing," panted Stew, "she's Mary...Mary Toh."

Wing reached the dock and leaped aboard a small boat. Her every action showed she was a professional. She moved quickly and precisely as she threw off the mooring ropes and started the motor. When Jim and Jonathan reached the dock, they could only see the back end of Wing's boat racing away.

Everyone jumped into Stew's boat, ready to give chase. It was larger than Wing's craft, but that made it more difficult to handle in the churning water. Stew started the motor, but wouldn't leave until everyone retrieved a life jacket from below and put it on.

"Mr. Priest, let's go," urged Ashley. "We *have* to catch her."

"Don't worry, we'll catch her," assured Stew. He settled into the captain's chair and pulled away. "You just make sure no one falls overboard. We shouldn't be out here in this weather."

Wing had a big head start. Her boat disappeared toward the center of the lake, hidden by the rain. Stew wasn't concerned, however. He knew he could make up the distance. His main concern was going too fast for conditions. He didn't want to collide with another boat.

"What will we do when we catch her?" asked Jim. He stared into the dark, misty clouds surrounding them, searching for Wing's boat.

"I guess we'll just turn her over to the authorities," said Jonathan.

"You kids better know what you're doing," said Stew. "As far as I know, that woman is Mary Toh. We won't look real smart if it turns out she's not Wing."

"She's Wing, Mr. Priest," said Jonathan. "Don't worry. Why else would she take off like that when she saw us? She knew we could identify her and blow her cover."

"She runs the whole smuggling ring," said Matthew. "She's the boss. Jim and I heard Roberts and Bongo

127

talking about it in the truck. We just assumed Wing was a man."

Stew couldn't chance going full speed. He realized Wing would be speeding flat out because she was running for her life. Though his boat was much faster, he couldn't open up all the way because of the low visibility. "I hate to tell you," he began, "but it's possible we aren't going to catch her. I can't see well enough to go fast. Maybe we should head back and tell the Mounties. They'll pick her up."

"Please don't turn back, Mr. Priest," pleaded Ashley. "Can we just keep going in case we find her? Where would she go?"

Stew loved the excitement that seemed to follow these kids around. But as the rain continued to pour and the waves grew larger, he faced the disappointing reality that they were probably wasting their time.

"I'm thinking this is a job for the authorities," he said. "This is their business...it's what they do, you know what I mean? Besides, as Matthew would say, with the weather getting worse, we're surfing close to the edge." His decision made, he turned the steering wheel and headed toward home.

Everyone felt sharp disappointment. Matthew's eyes were the saddest, and Jonathan thought his little brother might cry.

"Don't look at me like you think I'm going to cry, Jonathan," said Matthew. "It's just a bummer. We almost had it wrapped up. Geez, it feels just like when the Angels lost the World Series."

"But remember," said Stew, "there's always next year."

"Yeah, sure," replied Matthew, "and some day I'll be as big as everyone else. It's still a bummer."

"Don't forget that other saying," said Jim. "It ain't over 'til it's over."

"That's right," added Jonathan. "And it ain't over 'til the fat lady sings."

"That's not a particularly nice saying," said Stew. "Especially if you're a fat lady." He grinned.

As the boys laughed, Ashley went ballistic. "Why are you guys joking when we're giving up?" she asked, her voice louder than normal. "It's not funny. Why should we let her get away so easily?"

"Now, Ashley," said Stew, "don't be pigheaded about this. The police will catch her."

Jonathan grinned. "She's not pigheaded, Mr. Priest," he said. "She's determined. Dad taught us to be determined and persistent. He says people will call us stubborn. I guess he's right."

"Ouch!" squealed Ashley.

Stew instantly reacted to her apparent pain. "What is it, Ashley? What hurts? Jim, take the wheel." He held Ashley's shoulders and crouched so he could see her face. "What is it? Are you OK?"

For a moment, the others were worried, too. They were all surprised when Ashley's face lit up. "She's *here,*" she announced.

"Who's here?" asked Stew. "You'd better sit down for a

minute, girl."

At that instant, the sun broke through the clouds. The rain continued to fall, but less strongly. Stew looked at the sky. He'd lived in the Yukon his whole life and he'd never seen anything like it. The sky was full of dark clouds, yet there were no clouds in front of the sun.

"It's Leolin!" exclaimed Ashley. "It's the Inukin...I heard them talking!"

"All right!" yelled Matthew. "Turn this sucker around. We have a poacher to catch."

Stew didn't react so quickly. He was confused. He looked to Jonathan for an explanation. Jonathan smiled. "Like Jim says," he laughed, "it ain't over 'til it's over."

When Jim steered the boat back toward the center of the lake, Stew didn't object. He took the wheel, glanced at Jonathan and Ashley, and opened the throttle wide. The big boat took off with a jolt. "Let's go find us a bear killer," he said.

WING II

"Use the binoculars and watch the shore," Stew instructed. "I'm heading for Tagish Lake. If you see her boat on shore, we'll pull in." The boat was really flying now. They knew they had little chance of catching Wing—but at least they could try.

They soon closed in on the southern end of Marsh Lake. Going under the Tagish River bridge, they didn't slow down a bit. There wasn't another boat on the entire lake.

"We need to make a decision," said Stew. "Do we head west into Windy Arm, or south into Taku Arm? She could have gone either way."

"They're both part of Tagish Lake, right?" asked Jonathan. Stew nodded.

"How big is Taku Arm?" asked Ashley, her eye on the clouds.

"Thirty, maybe forty miles long," said Stew. "Long and narrow."

"Go there," instructed Ashley. "She went into Taku Arm."

"Aye, aye, sir," laughed Stew. "We go down Taku Arm." He was enjoying himself again. He loved these kids.

Fifteen minutes later they were still barreling down the lake at full speed, but there was no sign of Wing. Once, Matthew spotted a boat on shore that looked like Wing's, but it turned out to be only campers.

Stew was really into the spirit of things now. He knew these lakes like the back of his hand and he wanted the kids to succeed. They were depending on him.

"Damn!" he exclaimed. "I haven't had this much fun since one time with Red..." He paused.

"Since what time with Red, Mr. Priest?" asked Matthew.

"Uh...well...I guess I shouldn't say. It was a *great* time, though, let me tell you. I'll tell you about it when you're older."

"There you go again," said Matthew. "You're always

saying I'm too young."

"I don't want to interrupt your fun, Mr. Priest," said Ashley, "but I think I see her." She spoke calmly and held the binoculars steady. "I do. It's Wing. Straight ahead."

The tension on the boat rose to a high pitch as they closed in on their quarry. Wing was going at full

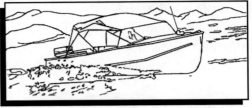

speed, but they narrowed the gap steadily. Finally they were close enough to recognize her boat with the naked eye.

"We have her," squealed Matthew, exchanging high fives with Jim and Jonathan. "You found her, Mr. Priest. You found her!"

Stew Priest couldn't hold back the smile creasing his face. He loved Matthew's infectious enthusiasm. "*Radical cool, dude,*" he yelled.

Wing wasn't in their pocket yet, however. She pointed something at them as they drew closer.

"Watch out," yelled Ashley, "she has a pistol!"

They ducked as several shots rang out. Wing was still a fair distance away, so Stew wasn't concerned as long as everyone stayed down. More shots cracked across the gap between the boats.

"That's it," said Stew. "Six shots. She'll have to reload. Let's go get her." He squeezed every ounce of speed out of his engine. They could see Wing wasn't reloading. She was just desperately trying to get away.

"*Whoo-ee!*" yelped Stew as they closed in. "I haven't had this much fun since..." He was interrupted by a loud grinding sound in the rear of the boat. The noise only lasted about two seconds, but that's all it took. The motor stopped dead.

"What the..." began Stew. He was in a state of shock. "What the heck..." He stared back at the motor compartment. All eyes were on him, but all he could see was a hatch cover under which lay the motor that cursed his life. "You dirty, rotten son of a..."

Ashley watched Wing through the binoculars as she pulled away from them once more. "She's laughing at us," she announced. "She's looking right at us and laughing her head off!"

Jim hopped down to the diving platform and lowered the small spare motor into the water. He yanked the cord and the motor came to life. The boat began to move slowly. Jim steered it so they again headed in Wing's direction. He could have gone in any direction and Stew wouldn't have noticed. He just stood at the wheel staring back down on the engine compartment.

Ashley and Jonathan realized Stew was in a quiet rage. "Don't worry, Mr. Priest," said Jonathan, trying to hide his disappointment. "It's not that big a deal. We'll be fine with the spare motor. At least we're not stuck without *any* motor at all."

"Every time," muttered Stew. "Every damn time!"

Clouds again blocked out the sun. Rain pelted down

with renewed vigor. As Wing's boat became a disappearing spot, Ashley looked at the sky. "Where are you, Princess Leolin...where are you?"

15

THE CATCH

The boat putted through the rain, going up and down more than forward. Stew regained his composure, but his zest had deserted him. "I'm too old for this," he said, wearily. "Should have retired in Arizona or New Mexico. Somewhere far from this boat."

"Maybe it's time to turn back," suggested Ashley. "We aren't going to catch Wing this way." She looked at Jim, who seemed intent on pursuing Wing in spite of the bad weather and their slow pace.

"I could phone the R.C.M.P.," said Matthew. "At least we'd have the satisfaction of telling them where she is."

"You could try the radio, Matt," said Jonathan, "but you can't phone anyone. The communicator is on the table in

135

the cabin. We left in a hurry, remember?"

Jonathan was right. Matthew's face filled with disappointment. He felt lost without the communicator. Stew caught his eye.

"No fun, is it?" asked Stew. "Going along, *boom, boom, boom*—and suddenly it's over. It's just you. No big, powerful motor, no fancy cellular-telephone communicator. No databases. No nothing. Just you. Alone."

"That's when you really start to have fun, though, isn't it?" said Ashley. "As long as you're not hurt, I mean. When things go wrong, you have to start again. It's like the rules change, and now you have to figure them out. You have to look at things differently, find a new solution. It's like a...a challenge."

Jonathan laughed. "We're motor challenged, I guess," he said.

"We're what?" asked Stew.

"We're motor challenged," said Matthew, giggling. "You're generically boat challenged, Mr. Priest. I'm communicator challenged. We're also weather challenged."

"What are you talking about?" asked Stew, grinning.

"Mr. Priest is understanding challenged," laughed Jonathan. "What do you think, Jim?"

Jim couldn't hold back a smile. He'd never met people like Ashley, Jonathan and Matthew before. They never let up. They just kept bouncing back. "It's my considered opinion," he said, "that Mr. Priest and those others currently aboard this normally great late-twentieth-century technological artifact, that is, the people on this useless boat, are in for a big surprise. Please observe we have company off the starboard bow."

They turned to look where Jim was pointing. Their laughter stopped. Wing's boat was rocking in the waves. It was dead in the water.

"I'll be darned," said Stew, springing back to life. Wing was sitting on a bench seat in the back of the boat. She wasn't laughing anymore. Jim steered toward her.

"Be careful, everyone," cautioned Ashley.

As it turned out, Wing offered no resistance as Stew and Jonathan boarded her boat. Stew checked the boat quickly, trying to see what had caused Wing to stop. There was plenty of fuel. He started the outboard motor and it roared to life.

"I don't get it," he said. "Everything works." He wondered why she stopped. "Why did you stop, Mary?" he asked. Wing looked at Stew with disdain. She obviously was in no mood to talk.

Stew put the motor in gear. Nothing happened. It kept running, but the boat didn't move. He could feel the mechanism engage when he shifted into reverse, but still nothing happened. He shut the engine down and yanked the shaft from the water. He saw the problem immediately.

"There's no prop," he said. "The propeller's gone."

"She must have hit something in the water," said Jim.

Stew shook his head. "No, Jim, she didn't hit anything. The propeller isn't broken. It's just plain gone. It's been removed. It isn't there and nothing's scratched."

Ashley, Jonathan, Matthew, and Jim looked at each

other. "Princess Leolin strikes again," yelled Matthew. "Nothing can stand in the way of the Inukin!"

As he was leaving the smaller boat, something caught Stew's eye. He picked up an object. "Well, would you look at this." He held the stone object for the others to see. "It's a scraper. An ancient Indian scraper. It looks exactly like the one you found on Bove Island, Matthew. I guess they aren't as rare as I thought." He handed it to Ashley.

"They're rare, Mr. Priest, believe me, they're rare. Take my word for it, you don't want this scraper in your hand...or your pocket...or anywhere else." She passed it to Jim. "I think this is yours, Jim."

Jim examined the scraper. He knew this was what Princess Leolin had intended him to find on Bove Island. Now he had it. Princess Leolin had won. Some day he might join his ancestors partying in the heavens. Perhaps he would challenge the unknown and end up joining Princess Leolin's band. He wasn't sure. But he was certain the Others weren't going to recruit him. He felt good. With a last look, he tossed the scraper into Tagish Lake.

Wing didn't say a word as they bundled her aboard. "Let's see how *you* enjoy being tied up," said Ashley.

"Cool it, Ash," said Jonathan. "We caught her, OK? She's not going to do any more harm." He was amazed how Wing got under Ashley's skin.

Ashley relaxed. Suddenly, she realized it was over. "It's over," she said. "We did it...we caught the mastermind!" Everyone celebrated—except Jim.

"What's wrong, Jim?" asked Matthew. "We did it!"

Jim was obviously as happy as the others that they had succeeded against the odds. But he wasn't prepared to celebrate just yet. "It ain't over 'til it's over," he said.

IN FOR REPAIRS

The next day a crowd gathered at the Priest's Marsh Lake cabin. Wing Toh had been turned over to the R.C.M.P. and she confessed to operating a poaching ring in Alaska and the Yukon Territory. It turned out she had four others like Roberts and Bongo working for her in Alaska.

Stew was holding court on the deck. "She wouldn't talk until they confronted her with the evidence found in the guest house," he said. Neighbors from miles around hung on his every word. "I still can't believe it was all happening right under my nose. She had a big-time operation going, that's for sure."

"What about Roberts and Bongo?" asked a reporter from Anchorage. "How did they get them?"

Stew was in his glory. "Caught 'em at the Juneau airport. They had just refueled and were about to head south when State Troopers picked them up."

Inside, Trudy was baking more bread. "I've never had so many visitors," she said. "Someone said more reporters just arrived in Whitehorse from California to interview you kids. Something about being on a talk show. They're on their way now. I can't stand it. They've already tramped all over my new lawn. Nobody seems to realize how hard it is to grow a good lawn up here." She was interrupted by a soft *beep beep.*

"Another fax, Matthew? How many is that today?"

"Yahoo!" cheered Matthew, as the fax rolled from the communicator. "We did it, Jim. They accepted our story about the underground dwelling at another newspaper. This one's in Toronto. That's six!"

Trudy joined Matthew and Jim. "Exactly how does that little machine work, anyway? You boys wrote that big story and sent it all over the world somehow. Where is all the stuff hiding?"

"On a storage medium," answered Jim. "Inside this machine are three types..."

"Just a second," interrupted Trudy. "Explain to me how it can print a perfect page, yet doesn't make a sound. Where's the...the...you know, all the machine parts? Look at my bread maker. It's fancy, but it's still a machine I understand. It has parts, know what I mean? Things. This little wonder doesn't have parts, so I can't understand how it works. It's like magic."

"Yeah, it is sort of like magic, isn't it?" said Jim.

"But it isn't magic," said Matthew. "The printer is a bundle of fiber-optic cables emitting light pulses that create heat and transfer an image to the page. Running it in reverse is how it sends a fax. Unless the fax is from an electronic file, then..."

"Whoa," interrupted Trudy, unloading another loaf of bread. "I can't understand something I can't see, that's all

I'm saying. I know it works, but I can't understand light particles or whatever it is. So for me, it's more like magic than anything. Of course, I know there's no such thing as magic...not real magic."

"Ouch!" said Ashley. "They're back. Princess Leolin, that hurts!"

"What is it?" asked Trudy, rushing to Ashley's side. "What's wrong?"

Ashley, Jonathan, Jim, and Matthew looked at each other, as if they were all thinking the same thing. They laughed.

"I'm fine, Mrs. Priest. I think I just received a stray fax in my ears," said Ashley.

"Here comes another one," announced Matthew. "It says the University of Alaska and the University of Moscow are sending a joint team to the Yukon to investigate the ancient underground dwelling. It asks if we're prepared to support them in this study? Way cool! We get to camp on Lake Bennett again."

"Look how it's addressed," said Ashley. "Congratulations, *Professor* Matthew Adams. Dad will be pleased with your progress. You, too, *Professor* Jim. Your school counsellor will be impressed."

Jim smiled and extended his hand to Matthew. "Pleased to meet you, *Professor* Matthew."

"Pleased to meet *you*, Professor Jim."

Stew swaggered in the door.

"How's the most popular man on Marsh Lake?" asked Trudy. "We've missed you. Have all the reporters left?"

141

"Nope," replied Stew. "I have to head into Whitehorse. Boat's going in for repairs. They figure it'll take a few days."

"That boat is soaking up all our retirement savings, Stew Priest," said Trudy. "We're going to have to get rid of it."

"I'll sell it, then," said Stew. He looked at Ashley and winked. Everyone knew the boat was more important to Stew than all the retirement savings in the world. "Anyone coming with me?" he asked.

The four slipped out the back door and clambered into the truck. Stew chuckled as they started down the dusty road.

"What's so funny?" asked Ashley.

"I figured out what's wrong with the boat," replied Stew. "Something you kids said set me to thinking and now I understand."

"Well?" asked Jonathan and Ashley.

"It's water challenged," said Stew, pulling onto the Alaska Highway. "This boat is water challenged!"

About the Author

David Skidd grew up in Eastern Canada and attended St. Mary's University, the University of Ottawa, and the University of Kansas. He has taught at Universities in the United States and overseas.

An avid reader and writer, David enjoys music, Northern living, and learning about different cultures and philosophies.

The *Alaska Highway Adventure Series* is David's first work for young adults. In these stories he combines mystery and adventure with the natural sense of wonder felt by all who love the North.

About the Cover Artist

Kate Williams is a noted artist who evokes her vision of the North primarily through fibre art and textile creations. She has studied in New Zealand and Nepal, pursuing her interest in traditional ethnic textiles. Her work is found in the Yukon Permanent Art Collection and in private collections throughout the North. Kate has recently expanded her scope to include printmaking and handmade paper creations.

Born in England, Kate moved to the Yukon in 1969 where she has been an art teacher since 1980. She enjoys adventurous